I0657539

# ♥ FATHER'S $ DAY

## a novel

## Gary Alexander

### The New Atlantian Library

# THE NEW ATLANTIAN LIBRARY
is an imprint of
## ABSOLUTELY AMAZING eBOOKS

Published by Whiz Bang LLC, 926 Truman Avenue, Key West, Florida 33040, USA.

*Father's Day* copyright © 2015 by Gary Alexander. Electronic compilation/ paperback edition copyright © 2015 by Whiz Bang LLC.

All rights reserved. No part of this book may be reproduced, scanned, or transmitted in any form or by any means, electronic or mechanical, including photocopying, recording, or any information storage and retrieval system, without permission in writing from the publisher. Please do not participate in or encourage piracy of copyrighted materials in violation of the author's rights. Purchase only authorized ebook editions.

This is a work of fiction. Names, characters, places, and incidents either are the product of the author's imagination or are used fictitiously, and any resemblance to actual persons, living or dead, businesses, companies, events, or locales is entirely coincidental. While the author has made every effort to provide accurate information at the time of publication, neither the publisher nor the author assumes any responsibility for errors, or for changes that occur after publication. Further, the publisher does not have any control over and does not assume any responsibility for author or third-party websites or their contents. How the ebook displays on a given reader is beyond the publisher's control.

For information contact:
Publisher@AbsolutelyAmazingEbooks.com

ISBN-13:978-0692559321 (New Atlantian Library, The)
ISBN-10:0692559329

# ♥ FATHER'S $ DAY

It is easier for a father to have children than for children to have a real father.

- Pope John XXIII

# In the Spring of Y2K

# 1.

For his 60th birthday, Joe Buckley bought himself an eatery. A robust man who looked younger, Buckley was healthier than he deserved to be. He had had a few nasty spots burned off his face and arms with liquid nitrogen and his urinary stream could no longer topple an anthill. That was it in the medical malfunction department.

Financial health was another matter entirely. Assets came to roughly $4800. His money would be gone long before he was. He had no old age security except his wits. Crossing into his definition of geezerhood got him to thinking: Better late than never.

So Joe Buckley purchased Molly's Restaurant on Burns Avenue, the main drag of San Ignacio, a hilly river town in western Belize, a 20- minute drive from Guatemala.

A favorite watering hole of his, Molly's was a cockeyed frame building half the size of a McDonald's. Ceiling fans paddled slabs of sticky air onto a rummage sale assortment of furniture. A porch and two benches fronted Burns, an easygoing gridlock of jaywalkers and vehicles. Utility lines crisscrossed above like extraterrestrial spaghetti and dogs snoozed where they pleased, displaying their ribs.

He didn't actually lay out any cash. Molly's consistently lost money and the owner was happy to walk away. Buckley wasn't the new legal owner either. He couldn't buy property in Belize. He didn't have the right papers, the story of his life.

Buckley went to Sharon Usher, a woman he used to

live with who was still speaking to him. She agreed to silent partnership when he promised she wouldn't have to lift a finger in the enterprise.

"I know about your promises," Sharon Usher said sourly as she signed.

Buckley figured he could make a go of Molly's and it'd be a turnaround of his life besides. He'd spent much of his adult life cooking and bartending, and had a policy of not drinking where he worked. Or at least cutting back. Under proper management, Molly's would be if not a gold mine a steady income Buckley could ride into the sunset, into his golden years.

Ecotourism in the area was on the increase too. Visitors could check out orchids and toucans, explore Maya ruins, and unwind at Molly's afterwards, eating and drinking. In fact, Buckley might just run a tour sideline out of the café, leading groups himself. He'd gained a superficial knowledge of the local archaeology and had become fairly sharp on the flora and fauna, a life list of 288 bird species under his belt.

From a barstool vantage point, Buckley had noted upgrades easily made. The food was okay, especially the breakfast omelets and the Wednesday night rice, beans and stewed chicken special. Just a little tinkering was all it'd take.

Squeeze a gift shop in the corner with the big table that was rarely full. Postcards, T-shirts, arts and crafts. He might even shell out for a computer and be a cybercafé, if somebody could show him how the damn things worked.

Buckley started by tending bar. He planned to roll up his sleeves and get involved in the kitchen too, a hands-on restaurateur. He considered and quickly rejected a name change. Buckley's sounded like a dry goods store, Joe Buckley's like a retired soccer player or a boozy expat, the latter hitting too close to home.

Molly's would remain Molly's. It was only a name anyhow. Molly had been three or four or five proprietors ago and nobody recalled who she was.

Two mornings into Buckley's entrepreneurship, he received a letter from Stan Buckley, his only child. Inside the letter was a smaller envelope.

"It's from my boy," he said. "First contact in ages."

"Want money?" asked Keith, Buckley's only bar customer.

The sky suddenly darkened. Lightning transformed the sky into a video game and thunder boomed like artillery. Rain fell as if a waterfall. In 15 minutes the sky would be blue, pavement steaming, the air smelling like laundry. The long, hot, wet summer. Which was slightly wetter and hotter than the long, hot, wet winter.

Buckley shook his head and raised his voice to compete with the sheeting on the tin roof.

"Nope. Not him. My ex-wife once said he liked computers. Computer people, they make damn good money."

"They don't write unless they want something."

The color and texture of old leather, Keith was older than Buckley, his full head of tightly coiled hair bleached white by years and the sun. He claimed to have been an iguana poacher, *chiclero*, deep-sea diver, faith healer, large appliance repairman, gigolo, Maya artifact smuggler and taxidermist. All Buckley had ever seen him do is pull odd jobs and drink.

Buckley and Keith had hoisted a few Belikin beers. From a server to customer perspective, Keith looked different. Face to face instead of side by side, he seemed off kilter.

Buckley opened the inner envelope and began dancing a lurching jig, waving the contents, a wedding invitation. "Stan's getting married. Jesus H. Christ, he's thirty-three or thirty-four and he's finally tying the knot. I'm invited to the wedding."

"Where at?"

"In the States, up on the northwest coast. Cannon Beach, Oregon. They're gonna perform the service right there on the beach. 'At our vacation home' he says. Him and his intended, they must have rented a beachfront cabin."

Keith asked for another Belikin. He didn't ask if Buckley was going to the wedding.

Buckley read on. The fancy scroll listed Mrs. Susan Johnson Buckley as mother of the groom, Mr. Charles Baxter and Ms. Irene Harris Baxter as parents of the bride, Elizabeth Ann Baxter. He hoped it was a good, decent, respectable family, a family good enough for his boy.

It'd be a reach, Buckley knew, to list Mr. Joseph Buckley as the father of the groom as he'd been a miserable, nonexistent dad. Susan keeping the Buckley name, that was a plus, though. After she unloaded Buckley, she'd accumulated other surnames to pick from.

The letter was typed on thick business stationery embossed with a logo consisting of "sjbWare" inside a leaning rectangle. It made no product sense, gave no hint of the boy's employer's line of business. There was no greeting, no Dear Pop, no Dear Mr. Buckley, no Dear Occupant/Stranger, no nothing.

Stan hoped he'd attend the wedding and understood if he didn't. "Mom suggested I offer assistance, airfare or other expenses, and I'd be happy to."

Yeah, Stan meant well, but the formal tone, the attitude, frosted Buckley. Essentially, the kid was saying he'd made good without a natural father. Not that Buckley could blame him for having that frame of mind.

"Gimme your take on this, Keith," Buckley asked, pointing at the logo.

"It's a parallelogram."

"What is?"

"The angled box around the printing."

"How'd you know that?"

"You accusing me of stupid on account of I know my parallelograms? I know my rhomboids and my triangulations too if you gotta ask. I used to teach arithmetic in a school up by Orange Walk."

"You're a customer," Buckley said. "All my customers are smart. I'm asking the meaning of the logo, what kind of business."

"It's printing inside a parallelogram," Keith said.

"Maybe it has to do with computers?"

"Computers," Keith said, staring dreamily at his Belikin. "I should of gone into computers."

By the next day, Buckley had pretty much decided not to go. How could he with his new business responsibilities? And there was the other thing hanging over his head.

He was ready to find a nice card to mail off when Susan, his ex, called.

"You're coming up in the world," she said. "The girl who answered said you were the boss."

How long since they'd spoken? He almost asked her how she tracked him down, but that'd be rude. "It's a living. You're sounding good, Sooz. Exactly the same."

Susan and Julie London were vocal twins. Susan's voice drove him positively goofy. Her on the phone complaining about the weather was twice as sexy as any 1-900 potty mouth.

"You a businessman. That's still sinking in."

"Better late than never."

"Well, good luck. Have you gotten Stanley's wonderful news?"

Stanley. Him and Sooz, they'd had a major beef

naming the baby. Stan, Buckley's brother, had been shot dead by police outside a bank he robbed. But Big Stan was alive when Little Stan was born, in the Oregon State Pen in Salem, doing seven-to-ten for another botched bank job. Were he dead *then*, the argument might've been less poisonous, the memory smoother to get past than the man. Honoring the deceased and so forth. Although Buckley won the battle, their son was always Stan*ley* to her.

"Sure did. Have you met the bride-to-be?"

"Of course. I live in the Seattle area, same as them."

How the hell would I know, Buckley didn't say. He'd've left himself wide open. "Approve of her?"

"Well, yes."

"That's not a very convincing well-yes. Has Stan known her long?"

"Beth works with Stanley."

"So what's this sjbWare outfit they work for?"

"Joe. Think. The initials."

sjb. Stanley Joseph Buckley. "Hey, his own company! He's a businessman too."

"Yes he is."

"A chip off the old block."

"Lord help him if he is."

"I betcha it's computers."

"An accurate guess. sjbWare markets a program that makes your operating system run faster and more powerfully, and you may not even know you have it."

"No kidding?"

"Technology, Joe, is a brave new world unto itself."

He'd worked with Susan when they met too. Buckley was the swing shift cook and she waitressed cocktails. "Good for them. Great. Swell."

"You are coming."

He wasn't certain if that was a question or a

command. Classic Susan. "It'll be rough to get away. There's a lot going on."

"If it's money."

"It's not money."

"If it's money, Joe, Stanley can help. Father's Day is upcoming soon too."

"We got a bad connection, Sooz? It's not money."

"Have you settled the, um, yet?"

The "um", "the other thing hanging over his head", was Buckley's desertion from the United States Army in 1966. He said, "You don't settle. You turn yourself in or you don't. It's a bit late in the ol' ball game."

"Buckley, you're not exactly Public Enemy Number One, you know. And isn't there a statute of limitations?"

"They may forget. They don't forgive. I get into the country and stopped and they punch my name into one of their computer machines, I'm a goner. Token jail time, which I'll get for the principle of the thing, at my age, it's a life sentence."

"At your age," Susan said. "At *our* age."

"You're like two years younger than me, Sooz."

"I'm no kid. That's what I mean. I've gone to college. I'm in a low-impact aerobics class and I'm studying feng shui. You're as old you feel, Joe. Happy birthday, incidentally."

Feng who? "Yeah, thanks."

Susan had been married and divorced four times he knew of. Him and her, they were youngsters from broken homes who also had in common 11th grade educations and white-hot hormones. He'd stopped matrimonial experimentation thereafter.

She improved herself financially on each marital cycle. Her most recent ex, if memory served, ran a body and paint shop. Or was it the tombstone engraver? No, he was before the body man and after the roofer.

"You'll get to meet Andrew."

"Andrew?"

"Andrew Cardigan is his name. We may be hearing wedding bells of our own. Andrew is an aspiring artist. Everyone says he's going to break out. He's incredibly creative."

"What kind of incredibly creative aspiring art are we talking about here?"

"Fine. Be snotty, Joe. That's the Joe Buckley I remember. Andrew paints in oils, acrylics, and is doing some daring experimentation in mixed media."

Daring. What the hell was wrong with a steady meal ticket like the body and fender guy? Maybe she was going through a second change of life.

"Sounds interesting."

"Try, will you, Joe. Please, please, please."

"I'll try."

"You've managed to cross into the country before."

"It's not that simple. I'd be going to Oregon, not spending an afternoon in a border town."

"Once you did your damnedest to look me up."

Buckley remembered. Him in San Diego, three rolls of quarters and a pint of Jim Beam in a phone booth, her on a honeymoon somewhere, him feeding the coin slot, babbling into answering machines. Ten years ago? "Uh huh."

"That was sweet."

"I'll try."

"How long since you've seen Stanley?"

Since the eighth grade, she knew good and well, rubbing it in. "Okay, I'll try."

"Our one and only child is marrying in three days, Joe. Try hard."

Buckley finished his shift behind the bar, opened a bottle of Belikin that was dripping sweat before his second swallow, and good-naturedly pestered his cook while he flipped burgers for a trio of backpackers. If he'd known being a businessman was so easy, so much fun, he'd've given it a fling sooner.

He walked to Sharon Usher's house. She lived a few blocks from Molly's, near the hospital where she was a nurse. She worked nights this month and was going out her door, dressed in white.

"Oh no," she said, almost colliding with Buckley. "Don't tell me."

Sharon Usher was a handsome, big-boned black woman in her fifties. Her husband and children were gone, and when Buckley moved in, it was as if she had taken on the burden of each again.

"I'll be gone only one week," he said. "My son's getting married this weekend."

"No."

"The only child I'll ever have."

"No."

Buckley fluttered a hand. "He's past thirty and unmarried. I really had to wonder about the boy, if you know what I mean. I'll tell you, I'm relieved."

"No."

"Molly's will run itself, Sharon, I swear. I've already got the place fine-tuned. You'll have to look in once in a while, be a pair of eyes. That'll keep the hired help in line, their paws out of the till. They're experienced employees. They know their jobs. Nothing to it. No sweat."

"No."

"One week, Sharon. One short week."

"A week?"

Buckley hugged her. "At the absolute maximum. I promise. And I'll stay in constant touch."

In spite of herself, Sharon hugged him back. "You and your promises."

*18*

# 2.

Buckley's adopted Belize, formerly British Honduras, the smallest country in Central America, was the area of New Hampshire and half as populous as Wyoming. Following independence in 1981, the Queen remained on their currency and their tongues, although Creole and Spanish poured forth as naturally, often all three languages in the same train of thought. Belizeans were the friendliest people in the world. Ask Buckley. He'd talk your arm off on the subject.

One Belizean in four lived in flat, steamy and ramshackle Belize City, which jutted into the Caribbean, as if sticking its chin out at Mother Nature, who periodically obliged. The federal authorities, weary of being pressure-washed by tropical storms, created an isolated, humdrum seat of government 50 miles inland. Belmopan was hurricane resistant, but not colorful, rough, charming, lively, raffish and exotic, as was (and is) its predecessor.

Most Belize City residents had no intention of moving. They were fatalistic. If something was gonna getcha, it was gonna getcha.

While Buckley liked the town too, he had no time to dawdle today. He caught a bus in, having already phoned Just Philip, who was waiting for him at the Texaco on Front Street by the Swing Bridge. Just Philip drove the mid-1980s, gunboat GM sedan favored by Belize City cabbies. Buckley climbed in, watching where he sat. The door trim and seats were more duct tape than not. Just Philip handed him a plump manila envelope.

"Keep 'em down on your lap," Just Philip said.

"I know the drill," Buckley said.

Just Philip dealt in lost identification. Buckley had never asked him to define "lost". Buckley sorted, weeding out the plump, the young, the swarthy. "Why do I have to do your job for you, Philip? You know me."

Looking through the rear-view mirror, Just Philip said, "Slow down. I have a number of IDs in your range. When a man reaches that age he has the means to travel. Stop. Yes, that is the best. It is fresh and crisp too, a matching driver's license at no extra cost. It's you, man."

Buckley looked at the thin, tanned face, thinner gray hair, and blue eyes of Harold Roy Qwerty of Colorado, USA. Buckley's scarring had blurred through the years and Qwerty's head-on photo rendered ambiguous the abuse Buckley's nose had taken in his youth. Those were the times when he learned that in barroom brawls, chairs don't bust into kindling like they do in the movies. And when you're thrown through a window, you come out the other side bleeding.

Buckley cut a fine line between ruggedly handsome and disfigured. His hair was thicker than Harold Roy's, and while he couldn't tell by the photo, Buckley was sure he had a flatter gut.

"What kind of name is Qwerty?" Buckley asked.

"Albanian. One of those countries over there."

"Albanians are named Harold?"

Just Philip said, "Ask Harold. Don't ask me."

"How long do you think I have on it?"

"How long you going for?"

"Maybe a week. My son's getting married."

"Longer than usual for you. You will be safe and secure for two weeks, bare minimum. Then Harold Roy gets to find his lost passport."

Buckley knew he'd asked the question wrong. If he'd said one year, Just Philip would've said two.

"This photo looks like me?"

Just Philip smiled. "You're his kid brother who played sports and scored on the girls. If challenged, say you were sick the day this was taken."

Buckley paid him. Just Philip rubbed thumb and forefinger together. "Another hundred Belizean."

Buckley gave him $50 U.S., the equivalent. "Since when? And for what, the flattery?"

"Since a long time ago. Inflation, man. Expenses."

Buckley had to think. A year this past spring. In an exceptionally busy tourist season, he slung hash and tended bar long hours, leaving little time to drink and otherwise piss away his wages. He'd gone to El Paso, a wad burning a hole in his pocket. While stationed at Fort Bliss, he had developed a liking for the El Paso dog track and the track across the border at Ciudad Juarez, liking the mutts, it proved, better than they liked him.

Philip was as black as coal and as thin as a red herring. He was about Stan's age. Buckley had been doing sporadic business with the man since Philip's late teens. Buckley once asked his last name and Philip had said he was just Philip, so he'd been Just Philip ever since.

"My son's getting married," Buckley said. "Up in Oregon. My son has his own business too."

"Let me ask you something and I'm not trying to scare off your business. Why not get your own ID? You're law abiding and you been creeping in and out of Belize longer than I been me."

Buckley's reasoning was uniquely Buckleyesque. He had legitimate Belizean identification, with which he traveled across borders, scrutinized like everyone else, but never investigated. It was in the States that Buckley worried. If detained for spitting on the sidewalk they'd run him in their fancy computers and bingo. There was an open warrant on deserters that did not go away, ever, even after death unless they were notified. He trusted that Harold Roy Qwerty had a tidier past.

"It's complicated," Buckley said.

"Your woes must be bad."

Buckley considered cadging a hop to the airport. Nope. It'd be his luck if they were pulled over, him and Just Philip and a car full of passports. He got out and said, "Not in my opinion they aren't. In my opinion I'm a solid citizen."

People regarding Buckley as a Vietnam deserter, that bugged him the most, he thought in the taxi as he practiced Harold R. Qwerty's signature. Only morons went over the hill in Nam. How the hell were you gonna get home when you were 10,000 miles of ocean away? Buckley took 30-days leave following his tour and didn't report for duty afterward. Vietnam wasn't the point anyhow. He'd spent an uneventful 12 months as a first cook in a Tan Son Nhut mess hall.

Born and more or less raised in a foothills logging town 60 miles out of Portland, Buckley had never known his father and everyone knew his mother. Buckley and his older brother ran semi-wild. Unlike Stan, Buckley avoided reform school. His offenses were, in his mind, trivial. Stolen hubcaps and fistfights and face-offs with parents who threatened broken bones and gunfire if he came near their daughters again. But nobody could tell him a damn thing either.

He'd been in the terminology of the late 1950s a juvenile delinquent. Back then, a judge tossed you in the pokey or booted your butt into the recruiting office, his call. You didn't have to be Charlie Starkweather. Look at Hissonor cross-eyed and he'd do to you what he felt like doing.

The Army put Buckley on a Boeing 707 and shipped him to Fort Ord, California for Basic Training, then made a cook out of him. They taught him to grill bulletproof pancakes, to cook spaghetti that was crisp and bacon that was not, and how to prepare vats of greasy, tasteless chow that made him think of witches and cauldrons.

When he went AWOL, Buckley had had seven years in, set to be a lifer. He'd re-upped for six more years in Saigon, a Burst of Six, they called it, and cashed a $1700 reenlistment bonus check. He realized on the long flight to the States that he'd be pushing 30 before pulling any more strings in his life.

It was late 1965. That advisor guano was coming to the end and they were shipping everybody and his brother to Southeast Asia to take over the war. Some were saying hell no, we won't go, burning their draft cards, skipping to Canada, and whatnot. Buckley had fulfilled his military obligation and then some.

Why, he even had on an upper arm as his one and only tattoo from his gung ho days a headless American eagle above a bannered UNITED STATES ARMY. The decapitated eagle was no unpatriotic affront, it was a circumstance that grew into a conversation piece.

So how come he couldn't quit like you did as a pump jockey at a gas station? Who the hell was he hurting?

Himself, that was for sure. In retrospect, he should have made his amends and taken his lumps. Susan came along. Stan came along. Before and after the divorce, Buckley drifted through a series of food service jobs where nobody did background investigations. The years raced by.

Eighteen of those years ago, a pantry chef on a cruise ship, making salads and sandwiches by the thousand, Buckley got into an altercation with the executive chef over a jar of mayonnaise too long unrefrigerated. This was the culmination of a feud that led to pushing and shoving, and beyond. The executive chef lost two teeth and scalded an arm on the steam table before the rest of the kitchen crew took Buckley down and sat on him.

They were anchored at San Pedro, at Ambergris Caye, close to the Belize Reef. Hotheaded Buckley was shown the gangplank. He hopped a water taxi to Belize City and eventually worked his way inland.

After seeing Just Philip, Buckley went to Belize International Airport and bought a round-trip ticket to Portland via Houston. Nobody hassled him. No rude questions, no contraband-sniffing pooches, nobody taking him into a room and snapping on a latex glove. Of a certain vintage, with a haircut, he was avuncular, almost dignified when need be. He fit no profiles. The aging Joe Buckley was practically invisible.

As he laid out his money at the ticket counter, he thought of the wedding present he still had to pick out and buy. He'd already stretched his budget thanks to Just Philip and his inflation. He could always cash in the ticket at the other end and take the bus home, to save a dollar or three.

While he waited at Houston for his Portland flight, he bought newspapers in every machine along the concourse. Not a particularly avid reader, Buckley craved newspapers. An American paper was difficult to find in Belize. His contact with the outside world was CNN, BBC World, and tourists, who invariably put their own editorial slant on things.

There was nothing unexpected, nor much good news. The business section was glum, with the NASDAQ and dot-com woes, all those technology stocks crashing and burning.

He'd long since lost interest in the fortunes of his favorite sports teams. None of the comic strips were familiar. When his plane boarded, he left a pile of papers for some lucky traveler, feeling as if he'd gorged himself and walked away from the table hungry.

Buckley's seatmate was a sleek, grayish-blonde in her forties. She wore a dark pants suit, businesslike perfume, and nothing on her ring finger. She lived in Portland, where she was a partner in a law practice.

"I own a restaurant in western Belize and am in the process of becoming involved as an archaeological guide at the Maya ruins," Buckley said, wishing now he'd washed the newsprint ink off his fingers.

"You lead a fascinating life, especially the archaeological part."

Buckley said it had its moments and launched into the history of Xunantunich and Cahal Pech ruins, laying on the big syllables.

"Of course, Caracol is the granddaddy on the Belize side, buried in the jungle," he lectured authoritatively. "You usually need a four-wheel-drive and don't even think about trying in the rainy season. I'll be honest. No Belizean ruin matches Tikal, in Guatemala, two hours from us. Then again, Tikal was under Caracol's thumb from 562 to 684 AD."

"Your profession makes a workaholic career in corporate litigation seem dull."

"It has its moments, like when you spot and identify a bird they've never before seen, such as a collared aracari or a Moctezuma oropendola or a citroeoline trogen. I'm a workaholic myself, especially in the dry season. Ever handle criminal cases against Uncle Sam?

She looked at him. "No, but an associate has experience in federal law."

Buckley saw that he had tripped an alarm and changed the subject. "I'm going to my son's wedding."

The attorney congratulated him and said that both her daughters married 18 months apart. She jokingly added that he was lucky to have a son since the bride's family traditionally bore most of the expense.

"A real financial blow for you and your husband, huh?"

"The girls' father's second wife has boys going to college this year and the next. He pleaded poverty."

"Everybody has an excuse," Buckley commiserated.

"Don't I know. Inside a deposition room and out."

Buckley asked for her business card. He didn't say why he wanted it and she didn't inquire. But she gave him one.

He rode a bus into downtown Portland, studying Dorothy L. Magnuson of Cline, Sedgwick, Holmes and Magnuson, attorneys at law. Not bad, even if she was the caboose. He wondered what she went by. Dorothy, probably, or Ms. Magnuson, although she didn't seem like a ballbuster. She didn't strike him as a Dot either.

If she'd asked his name, he'd probably said Hal. Harold Roy Qwerty may or may not go by Hal, but at the moment Buckley had felt like a Hal.

As Joseph J. Buckley, he had a resident alien Belize passport, an expired Belizean driver's license, an American Social Security card, and a Monterey, California library card, acquired while he was stationed at Ord and so tattered that it was virtually unreadable. He had stashed that documentation in the lining of his dilapidated Samsonite.

He got off where he thought the YMCA was. It wasn't. When last in Portland, everybody was getting out of the trolleys and into their cars. Now there were light rail coaches and he nearly stepped in front of one as he gawked at skyscrapers.

He bought more newspapers and took a room in a cheap hotel, staying in to stay out of mischief. Except for no ceiling fan, it wasn't unlike his rented room in San Ignacio. Unable to concentrate on rising electricity prices, Oregon highway repair costs, and baseball box scores, Buckley lay on the bed, imagining prospective grandchildren he thought he'd never have. Happy, healthy tykes, half a dozen or so. He'd work at being a long distance granddaddy if they'd let him.

He tried to recollect when he'd been a father to Stan, a bona fide father, a daddy, reading a bedtime story and tucking him in, giving him his allowance, taking him over his knee, any of that.

Susan and he had split the sheets when Stan was in grade school, and he'd been a largely absent figure prior to the formalities, working long shifts and/or fooling around. Any actual fathering was hazy. Afterward, he'd been sloppy on correspondence and birthdays, carrying on the Buckley tradition of cruddy parenthood.

Buckley and brother Stan hadn't known if they had separate fathers, and no man came forward. If their mother knew, she wasn't talking. Buckley had thought that she might finally spill the beans someday, maybe on her deathbed. But she belted down her last drink in a motor court on Highway 20, all alone. The John Smith who rented the unit had panicked and checked out through a window.

He remembered Stan as smart and inquisitive, asking the "how high is up?" kind of questions that stumped him. The youngster counted on his fingers and then on paper before he was in kindergarten. A nonathletic, congenial kid who entertained himself with a book or his own quiet thoughts, he acquired those traits elsewhere in the gene pool, from some long-lost shirttail relative.

Buckley discovered the birds and bees in his early teens. However, he didn't make the link from sex to reproduction to a living, breathing, happy family. Family was a word he defined in an angry stammer. The television Jim Andersons and Ozzies and Harriets and Ward and June Cleavers added to his confusion. The sweetness was incomprehensible. They might as well have been flying saucer people. Buckley could not picture Ward playing hide the salami with June. Nor Wally doing his homework to please the old man.

These days, dysfunctional is what they tagged families like his. Not nuclear, not stable, and no family values anywhere in sight. That was gonna change too. Yes sir. If he was going to turn his life around, he was gonna fix the dysfunctioning between him and his boy in at least some small way.

No doubt prodded by his mother, Stan/Stanley had opened that door a crack.

But how to proceed?

How?

Buckley stared at the ceiling, a squadron of butterflies launching in his stomach.

# 3.

Next day, wedding day.

Buckley caught a bus to the coast. He felt comfortable on buses. Without credit cards and a valid driver's license, it would be easier for him to steal a car than rent one. In tiny Belize, buses ran went everywhere and everybody rode them, old U.S. school district surplus where on the budget lines chickens had the run of the aisles.

He wondered if Stan had had a bachelor party. An all-night poker game and cigars. Dirty movies, a keg of beer, a cutie popping out of a cake.

Ah hell, the present!

Buckley got off in Astoria, a quaint town of restored Victorians on Oregon's northwest tip. He wished he'd grabbed something at an airport gift shop.

What might Stan want, this grown man who'd made good? Better yet, what had he liked as a kid? Buckley went into an antique store and, bingo, there it was, an old Schwinn, a single-speed, built like a tank. It was even maroon, a dead ringer for the bike Buckley had desperately wanted as a kid himself, but never got.

Susan had phoned him years ago. He was in Reno, if memory served, a breakfast line cook at a hotel, cracking so many eggs he dreamed about them. Christmas was coming up and she needed another fifty bucks for a ten-speed Stan just had to have. Buckley coughed up the fifty, visualizing her and her latest flame putting it together out of the box the night before.

"How much?"

"It's marked down to one hundred-and-ninety-five

dollars," the proprietor said.

"Needs a paint job and new grips."

The shopkeeper was a lard-butt Buckley's age, who tied what hair he had into a ponytail. He said blankly, "It is, after all, an antique."

Normally live and let live, Buckley was vaguely offended by the guy. He reminded him of the old expat hippies infesting Belize, burnout cases sporting the same dazed expression, as if they'd woke up five minutes ago puzzling where they'd been since 1971.

Buckley bargained hard, knocking the lard-butt down to $175, and went across the street to a drug store for a roll of ribbon. Exuberant and unsteady, he half-walked, half-rode to the bus stop. It was a sunny, lukewarm day, hardly in the 60s, frigid by San Ignacio standards, but perfect for outdoor nuptials on the Oregon coast.

He waited a few minutes and checked his watch. Two o'clock and the wedding started at four. Punctuality wasn't Buckley's long suit. He had no idea when the next bus was coming, so he stepped off the curb and extended a thumb.

Seemed like every other car they drove in the States these days wasn't a car. They were trucks and vans and SUVs. The third one of those monsters that came along stopped for Buckley, a harmless geezer, an old man with an old suitcase and an old bicycle.

Buckley stowed his bike and mangy suitcase in the bed of a dented Ford pickup that pumped out a rooster tail of blue smoke when the kid at the wheel pulled away. He wore a rock band T-shirt, a baseball cap on backwards, and an earring. He had barbed wire tattoos on each arm, approximately where Buckley's headless eagle was.

The United States of America had definitely changed. Everywhere you looked, young people were decorated like comic books. Earrings too, all over their faces for Chrissake sake, boys *and* girls. As far as he was concerned there were two valid reasons for having tattoos.

Number one, you were a biker. Refuse and the rest of the pack would toss you off a bridge. Second, an active military serviceman or a military veteran. You were out on pass and had a little too much to drink, you woke up in the morning tattooed. It tended to happen.

"What are you looking at?"

"Nothing," Buckley said, still giving him the once-over.

"*Grapes of Wrath*," the kid said, giving Buckley the once-over.

"Excuse me?"

"They made us read it in our junior year."

Kids, Buckley thought. They have their own language. Always had, always will.

For an hour, until Buckley signaled him to stop, he kept a cell phone pressed to his ear, calling one person after another, unnerving Buckley when he'd take his eyes off the road to dial. The conversations were boring with long uh-huh, uh-huh interims. The poor kid was getting an earful.

He dropped Buckley off at the first Cannon Beach cutoff road, which wound down a shallow hill. He mounted the Schwinn and coasted, suitcase balanced on handlebars, arms out, a 1950's pipsqueak again until a bump nearly sent him ass over teakettle.

Cannon Beach in his recollection had been a rustic seaside burg inhabited by the laid back. It had since been cutesyfied and spiffed up and touristed to the gills. Wine shops, art galleries, espresso, BMWs.

Buckley pedaled to the visitor center and spruced up in the men's room. He toweled off sweat and rolled on deodorant. He broke out a clean pair of slacks and a *guayabera* that was white as snow. He gave his shoes a quick spit shine. It was ten minutes till four.

He rushed from the can, fished out Stan's letter, and

asked the lady on duty where the address was. "I'm late for a wedding."

"Oh," she said, "that's the Buckley wedding."

*The* Buckley wedding.

Said the proud father, "Stan Buckley's my boy. My son."

"Really." She looked at him funny, but did give directions.

Buckley pumped hard, crossing the main drag, ignoring horn-honking traffic. Buckley's imagined cabin turned out to be a two-story colonial Molly's could fit inside of, so new the cedar siding hadn't faded to gray. Renting it for the occasion must've cost them a pretty penny.

On the beach behind it was a squarish, candy-striped circus tent, big enough for Ringling Brothers. Buckley glanced at his watch: 4:03. Shit.

He wound the ribbon around the Schwinn's seat, tied a bow of sorts, and trudged through dry, deep sand. Two or three hundred people at folding chairs inside the tent were standing. Some heads were cocked at him. They were in shorts and swimsuits, barefoot as often as not. For once in his life Joe Buckley was overdressed.

From the first row, Susan waved. A tad heavier than he remembered, though looking damn good. She had nothing to be ashamed of in her one-piecer. Plenty of that big hair he loved too, piled high, but it shocked him to see it solid silver. Her big green eyes sparkled. Or was that tears?

Only the bride and groom and preacher and a middle-aged lady were formally dressed for the occasion. In this setting they struck Buckley as ornaments you'd stick in the top of the cake.

Stan had a pot and a receding hairline. He gave his erstwhile father a bland nod and slipped a ring on Beth's finger.

Beth was a serious girl with a perm, rimless glasses, and a decent body. The preacher spoke and Buckley couldn't hear because of distance and the surf.

By the time he reached the tent, his boy was kissing his brand-new wife.

It made Buckley feel both good and bad that they'd been waiting on him. He wiped his eyes with a forearm as instant before Susan hugged him.

"Getting sentimental and sensitive in your dotage?"

"That's me."

"We hoped but did not really and truly believe we'd see you."

"Ye of little faith," Buckley said.

She laughed and introduced the man at her side. Andrew Cardigan was a beanpole, exceedingly hairy except for a pink face and shaved head. Buckley guessed 35 to 40. Buckley didn't recall Susan acquiring a taste for ratty young stuff.

"An international fugitive," Andrew said. "Outstanding. Send my regards to Robert Vesco."

Susan pinched what midriff flesh she could and said, "Andrew blurts what's on his mind. His paintings exhibit the same spontaneity. That's why he's going to be great, eventually adored internationally."

Buckley didn't reply. Where the hell did she come up with words like "dotage" and "spontaneity"?

"What's it like to kill, to casually extinguish a life?" Andrew went on. "Is it like they're a living homo sapiens or is it merely business, the commerce of armed conflict?"

"Huh? Kill who?"

"Oh for God's sake, Andrew. I told you, Joe was a cook in Vietnam."

"And presently a restaurateur and chef, I understand."

"A cook."

"What, may I ask, do you cook?"

"Food," Buckley said.

"Does Belizean cuisine share Mesoamerica's pre-Columbian culinary roots, the triad of beans, corn and squash?"

"My Renaissance man," Susan said.

"Sure," Buckley said. "My Wednesday night special is rice, beans and stewed chicken."

"What heat quotient?"

"Optional. We leave the hot sauce on the table. But I make an habañero salsa that'll bring you to your knees."

Andrew launched into a lecture on the habañero, the world's hottest pepper, the fieriest variant of the Scotch bonnet. While the capsaicin count on the overrated jalapeño registers a wimpy 3000 on the Scoville scale, the habañero begins at 100,000 Scoville Units and can exceed four hundred thousand. Et cetera, et cetera.

Buckley had nothing further to say to or hear from this smarty-pants.

He turned to Susan. "Do you like her? Beth?"

"Stanley does. That's the important thing." She gently kicked a Schwinn tire. "Cute idea. Is it for him or her?"

Good question. "They can take turns or she can ride on the handlebars."

Buckley noticed the fully clothed lady behind Beth, looking in their direction. She wore a pants suit too heavy for the weather and a face that indicated constipation.

Buckley smiled at her. She glared at him, then stared into some middle distance.

"That's Irene, mother of the bride," Susan said into his ear. "Turn off the Buckley charm. You're a male of the species. She'd prefer to march you all into the gas chambers. See over by the bar, pedophile and victim?"

Buckley had seen them, especially her. A blonde, dimpled, bikinied sweetie-pie, with a plump rosy-cheeked fella not a lot younger than himself. There was a fair amount of giggling and touchy-feely.

"Father of the bride and trophy wife. Chuck and Heather. In his former life he was Charles," she said. "C'mon. We're going to buck the receiving line."

Susan's hand was strong and dry. Was she still working, serving drinks to drunks? She had the legs and the stamina, but he hoped she wasn't.

She waded in and buried her son in teary smooches, then gave the bride a formal, cheek-grazing hug. Buckley clasped a hand that was not strong or dry, unsure what to do or say next. Stan would be taller than his father if he'd stand up straight, but a stoop built into his posture brought them to eye level.

"Good to see you," said Stanley Joseph Buckley. "Glad you could make it."

"Thanks. Glad I could," he said, then exchanging tight smiles with Beth.

Cordialities apparently completed, Buckley moved through to another table laden with food, plastic wrap peeled back, and a bar serviced by a bare-chested kid in a black bow tie. Other catering employees were folding chairs as a dance combo set up.

Buckley stood out of the way, watching his son greet guests, allotting them neither more nor less time and warmth than he had his father. Susan appeared with two glasses, red stuff on the rocks.

"Wine punch," she said.

They toasted and she asked, "What do you think of Andrew?"

"Very bright. Are the kids planning on having kids?"

"Is that a grandfatherly instinct I'm hearing?"

Buckley shrugged. "Grandchildren hadn't occurred to me."

That somehow pissed her off. "How could they when you think of nobody but yourself?"

Susan's minefield temper. You never knew where to step, but it didn't bother him. Not his problem. He looked at Andrew, who was schmoozing with band members, one eye on Buckley.

"Take your licks, Sooz. You been saving them up."

She finished her drink and caressed his arm, raising his sleeve. "Okay, no more shots. Just a dab of free advice."

"That's the most expensive kind."

"Clear things up with the Army."

"I will."

"No, you won't, and you know why?"

"I bet you're gonna tell me."

"It'd require growing up, giving up life on the edge. No more traipsing around carrying a wallet stuffed with phony ID, no more hiding out in banana republics, no more stupid thrills, no more free love, no more irresponsibility. You're getting too too old for this nonsense, Joe Buckley."

The music began.

"You oughta have one of those radio call-in shows," Buckley said. "Or write a book on how you're supposed to live your life."

She held on to his sleeve. "Your tattoo's faded and still decapitated."

"Never was capitated," Buckley said. "You still writing your diaries?"

"Each day faithfully. Okay, compulsively."

Buckley stroked his tattoo, overlapping to her hand. "You stayed up half the night after taking a gander at this."

"Our first night," she said. "Not to mention the implications of a work in progress interrupted by the news of President Kennedy's assassination."

"Strange times," Buckley said.

"Is there anybody serious in your life, Joe?"

"I'm playing the field at the moment."

"What else is new? Let's dance."

As Buckley kicked off his shoes, he saw black oystercatchers on the beach, out by the rocks. Bird species 289 on his life list.

"Thank you," Susan said.

"You haven't forgot my two left feet," he said, holding her, looking beyond her shoulder at Andrew, genius artist and know-it-all.

"Well. The bride and groom ought to be dancing the first dance, but they're nowhere in sight."

It was a slow tune.

"What the hell," Buckley said, pulling her in.

They finished. He asked for the next one and they danced even closer.

"Are we making up?" he asked.

"I do believe so. That or the punch is kicking in. Whichever, the tension's gone. I don't want to bash your noggin in with a chunk of driftwood anymore."

"I'd be nice to make up the way we used to."

She ground a gritty toe on his foot and stuck out her tongue. "Not a chance, buster."

Jealous grin plastered on his face like a decal, Andrew cut in on the third dance. Stan and Beth had returned. They'd changed into matching shorts and tops and sat by themselves at a tent flap. Buckley stood alone on the other side, like a wallflower at a sock hop. Father and son made occasional eye contact, but there was no movement.

Beth and Mama Irene were conferring, and Buckley made an unsuccessful eye contact attempt in that area too. Irene wouldn't be a bad looking lady if she'd quit being a sourpuss. Buckley hoped her bitterness and the father's shenanigans wouldn't carry over into how Beth took to married life.

The combo's beat picked up at sundown. Sand was flying. Buckley drank more punch. It was tasty and sneaky.

Somebody started a beach fire. The musicians and dancers moved out to it. Buckley retrieved his ex-wife for the fastest numbers. She was right about him, of course. Molly's should've been churning in his brain every waking minute. But it wasn't. He'd handed off the responsibility and that was that.

*Good to see you. Glad you could make it.*

Could've been worse. The boy had every right to spit in his eye.

What else he had in his wallet besides fake ID was Dorothy L. Magnuson's business card. He'd stop by Portland on his way to the airport. To ask for a date and/or for help on his Army situation. Which, he'd decide later. Maybe both.

Right now he and his ex were swinging their hips and elbows, sweating like racehorses. Shaking their booties, yeah, dancing to the music.

# 4.

Buckley was having a dream where he knew he was dreaming, but couldn't for the life of him wake up. While stationed at Fort Lewis, he'd been sent TDY (Temporary Duty) to Fort Wainwright, Alaska, near Fairbanks. It had been a February, the four coldest, most miserable weeks of his life.

Mess hall kitchens were always too hot, and Wainwright's was a blast furnace when you came in, but you ventured outside into the planet Pluto. This was a passive travelogue of a dream. Buckley replayed nothing of the people, the duty, the place, no details except that when you spit and it froze before it hit the ground, it was colder than -50°. He watched through a pane as every troop at Wainwright, from commanding general to buck private, spit on a parade ground, frozen saliva balls bouncing like hailstones.

Susan pummeled Buckley awake. "Joe, stop spitting in my hair."

"Uhhh."

Buckley cracked his eyelids. He wasn't in Alaska. He was in Cannon Beach, Oregon, on the beach, in a sleeping bag with his former wife, freezing his butt off. Raising to an elbow with difficulty, he listened to the roaring surf and squinted at a bluish gray sky, morning's first light. The cool, dampness reminded him that after 18 years in the tropics, his blood was thinner than broth.

He touched an aching hand to his aching head. "Ow, ow, ow."

"After last night, I should think 'ow'." Susan unzipped

the bag. "Be a dear and get my clothes. They're hanging on that driftwood snag behind us."

Buckley crawled onto the sand. He clung to the driftwood, raising ever so slowly to his feet, every joint in his body feeling its 60 years. He again vowed to cut down on the drinking and the accompanying bad decisions.

"Get dressed too, Joe."

"Huh?"

She laughed. "Buckley, standing there like that, naked as a jaybird, I hate you."

"For a new reason?"

"Because you still have a nice tush and decent abs. *Please* put something on before kids coming out to build a sand castle see you and get us arrested."

Buckley flexed his hands. They were skinned, the cartilage creaky. Arthritis was right around the corner. He handed Susan her swimsuit and shirt. As he aimed an unsteady foot into a trouser leg, he saw a blood streak on his *guayabera..*

Not given to probe every little pain and upset, Joe Buckley presumed from the git-go. his body would inform him of a misfire by knocking him flat on his backside. But blood he took seriously.

"Sooz, am I bleeding? Was I bleeding?"

She dressed inside the bag and said, "It isn't yours."

An ideal time to discontinue the topic. Buckley stepped into his shoes. He wished he still smoked.

"I wish I still smoked," Susan said, sitting up, buttoning her shirt over her swimsuit. "When did you quit?"

While married, they shared a scary telepathy. "Eleven years ago I woke up and couldn't stop coughing. You?"

"Mr. Sensitive. I threw away a half pack of Winstons when Stanley and I killed the rabbit, and haven't lit up since. You brought me flowers and said you'd quit then too. Right."

He helped her to her feet. "Better late than never."

"How are your knuckles?"

"Fine."

"You flinched."

"I'm piecing it together. Andrew was in my face, yelling, shoving." Buckley's voice tailed off.

"Andrew pushed between us when we dancing."

"What song?"

"*Unchained Melody*. You made the request."

"Yeah," Buckley said, nodding, shuffling his feet and humming the sultry lyrics. "We loved that song. Our song."

"Andrew said, and I quote, we were engaging in simulated intercourse."

A fragment flashed back. Buckley telling Andrew that if they were dryhumping, he'd sure as hell know it, him and everybody else. Something to that effect.

"I am not proud of myself, Joseph J. Buckley. Perhaps they should've thrown a bucket of cold water on us. Andrew had every right to call me the names he called me. Us."

"What names?"

"Names I won't repeat in mixed company."

"Aw hell, Sooz. I ruined the wedding."

"No, Joe. *We* ruined the reception, assisted by Andrew. You and I make quite a team. You avoid relationships. I botch them."

Buckley gritted his teeth and clenched his sore fists. "One of these days I'm gonna stop stepping on my own pecker."

"I'm not saying you weren't provoked."

"The blood?"

"You told him to stay down. He jumped up and tore into you again."

Buckley recalled the black oystercatchers by the rocks,

but not the blow by blow. Maybe Andrew had gotten in a lick or two, rattling his brainpan. He stretched, not without a twinge or three. "Jeez, I'm really sorry, Sooz."

She hooked a hand around his arm and steered him toward the house. "Buckley, you have a knack for bringing out the white trash in me."

"Always happy to be helpful."

"I'll wager that you haven't been in a brawl for years. At your age."

Actually months, if you were splitting hairs. He'd been tending bar up the street from Molly's. A loud, red-faced, pot-gutted Buick-GMC salesman from Houston would not leave the waitress alone, even after both she and Buckley asked politely. When he grabbed her ass, Buckley grabbed him by the ears and flattened his nose on the bar. It technically wasn't a fight, it was discipline. A lesson in manners, in saloon etiquette.

"Yep," Buckley said. "Years. Years and years. The kids weren't still there, were they?"

"The crowd had thinned out, including them, thank God. Irene too. Her and I, I have the feeling we're not gonna be warm and fuzzy moms-in-law."

"No tea parties knitting booties for the grandkids?"

"There you go again about grandchildren, you old softy."

"Where is Andrew?"

"He caught a ride to Seattle. His exit involved more name-calling."

"Well, hell, Sooz. I really am sorry."

"I did it to myself. I have this gift. Evidently I'm going home alone. Give you a lift?"

"On the plane, I met a prominent Portland lawyer who might take my case against the Army."

"Will wonders never cease."

"You can drop me there. I'll get to the airport afterward."

"This is Sunday, Joe."

"My attorney's a workaholic."

Buckley's suitcase was at the side of the house where he'd left it. They tiptoed inside to an open-beamed, high-ceilinged great room that reminded him of pictures of Hermann Goering's hunting lodge. Semi-comatose guests had flopped willy-nilly on any flat surface and some that weren't. Those awake, at the sight of Buckley, closed their eyes and feigned sleep.

They cleaned up in separate bathrooms, Buckley avoiding the train wreck in the mirror. They went to the laundry room, which was larger than Buckley's room in San Ignacio. Susan told him to take the shirt off and nothing else.

"*Guayabera.*"

"Off with it."

She rubbed goo out of a tube on the bloodstain and completed the load with dirty clothes in his suitcase. Everything came out like in a detergent commercial. Buckley loved the temporary domesticity.

They walked across the main street and wolfed down heaping plates of hash browns and hotcakes and eggs. Buckley had a side order of bacon and cup after cup of corrosive black coffee. He reached for the check, patted his midsection, and said that he might just survive now. Susan called him a human tapeworm and bottomless pit, like she used to.

They left in a gigantic SUV. Buckley rode as high as in a bus, and a lot smoother. The dashboard had wood trim and buttons galore. Leather seats made it smell like a shoe store.

"Yours?"

She hesitated. "Stanley's."

"He really is doing okay, huh."

"Oh yes."

"You told me his company makes this gizmo that

soups up computers. What's it look like?"

"Stanley invented sjbBoost and it doesn't look like anything."

"How can a thing not look like anything unless it's invisible?"

She cupped a hand. "It isn't a physical entity, Joe. It's software, a program preinstalled on your hard drive."

"So it is something."

"A program is coded instructions on silicon chips. It's a zillion zeros and ones opening and closing. Itty-bitty electrons."

Buckley threw in the towel. "You, Sooz, you're really doing okay?"

"I graduated from community college this spring. I plan to start at the University of Washington this fall."

"That's great. I'm happy for you," Buckley said, meaning it. "What are you taking?"

"English. History. Sociology. My major's up in the air."

"English," Buckley said. "Are you reading those romance novels? Take more English and you'll be able to write them. You know plenty of ten-dollar words already."

"Besides my diaries, the bodice-ripper genre is my only confessed addiction. I'd like to fit in the time to commit to running. I have a girl friend who competes in 10K's and half marathons."

Buckley did not run unless someone was chasing him. "You can iron things out with Andrew, can't you? If you want."

She looked at him. "I want. I do want. Don't get any boy-girl ideas. Last night was auld lang syne and a stupid mistake I thought I'd outgrown."

"Not me," Buckley said. "No ideas."

"Please fasten your seat belt, Joe. It's the law. This isn't the Third World."

Buckley buckled up and said, "Belize is poor, but it's

not the Third World, not in my opinion. Know why?"

Susan shook her head.

"Belizeans for the most part respect and obey their laws, and each other. They don't have coups. They don't disappear people."

Susan smiled. "An obviously tolerant nation to give you a home."

"Look, Sooz, anything I can do I'll do. I'll phone Andrew up, write him a letter, apologizing up one side and down the other. I'll offer to pay his doctor bills if he has to go in."

"You'd pay them?"

"No, but I'd offer to."

"That's sweet, but how would you handle what happened with us later on?"

"I'd lie like a rug. I'd lie through my teeth. I'd lie and swear on a stack of Bibles. I'd take an oath that all we did was walk the beach, talking about old times and the future, how much she loves you for all eternity and then some, yak yak yak."

"Andrew is no fool, Joe."

"Yeah, he's very bright."

"Andrew is pedantic, as you know. He has a temper and what might be considered a mean streak. Frustration causes his flare-ups. He's been so so close to making it as an artist. He's never had the right break."

"A temperamental genius artist."

Susan slowed. "I could let you out here."

"Sorry. You'll win him over. I know you will. Everybody makes mistakes."

"This was a doozie."

Buckley supposed it was a doozie and he knew all about doozies. He had no comforting response. Susan accelerated. She drove fast, always had. He didn't realize how fast until he glanced at the speedometer: 80 on a two-lane highway. This SUV, it was a rolling, supersonic living room.

"The honest truth, Sooz, whose idea was it to invite me to the wedding, Stan's or yours?"

"Stan*ley*'s or mine. The decision evolved from consensus. I thought it would be a fitting moment for father and son to stick a toe into each other's lives. How do you think it went, by the way?"

"Cordially."

"That was my impression too. By nature, he isn't demonstrative or extroverted. How what we did filters down to him will be crucial. When you get home, send Stanley a thank-you note. He'll send you one for the present. Play it by ear how it goes from here on."

"Good advice," Buckley said. "What was his part in the consensus evolving?"

"I'll be frank. I did most of the talking. You weren't on the long guest list, let alone the pruned-down short list."

"I don't blame him for hating me."

"He doesn't hate you, Joe. He doesn't know you. You aren't even an acquaintance, a blip on his screen. You don't exist."

"Ouch. He said okay to you like instantly?"

"No. The next day. Stanley is deliberate. He thinks everything through. After sleeping on it, he decided your presence was important enough that he wrote a letter with the invitation."

"Special treatment, huh?" Buckley said, eyes widening.

"Kind of. Stanley can be opaque. You have to read between the lines. My theory is that the suggestion started an itch he had to scratch, which I should have seen coming. You know my father died of a heart attack while we were still married. My mother passed away two years ago of emphysema in a nursing home. Weren't you curious why Mother wasn't at the wedding?"

"Yeah, I was," Buckley lied.

"That's fine, Joe. She didn't like you either."

"She warned you about me," he said.

"And did I listen? Stanley has no siblings due to a cyst two years after he was born and my hysterectomy. My two older sisters live in Arizona and Illinois. We exchange Christmas and birthday cards. Sometimes. They may or may not have gotten a card or gift to Stanley and Beth."

"I'm not following you, Sooz. Your sisters hate me too?"

"They didn't know you well enough. The point I'm finally getting to, despite interruptions, is that Stanley, new husband, prospective father —"

"He is?"

"Not yet. Those are my words." Susan sighed. "I'm assuming he will be a father eventually. He's curious about his origins. My family is an open, dull book. The Buckley side, on the other hand, is an itch he's scratching."

"Unknown father, troubled mother, brother gunned down by cops, and me with my Army situation."

"Stanley gave me the third degree on what's you've been up to. He hasn't asked about you since he was in high school. He knows more about your brother than I do. I was shocked. He has microfiche newspaper clippings of his bank robberies."

"Big Stan was a lousy bank robber," Buckley said. "He was not suited to a bank heist career."

"I think Stanley is building the Buckleys in his mind as the James Brothers or the Daltons."

Buckley laughed.

"That was my response too. The other factor in the invitation is you turning sixty. You're the last of the notorious Buckleys. You won't be around forever. He needed to see you in the horseflesh. Of course I'm speculating."

"You know him. You're probably on the mark."

"I'm sorry if I'm being too blunt, Joe."

Buckley shrugged. "Better than no interest at all."

"This lawyer is in downtown Portland?" Susan asked. "We're entering the county."

Buckley fished out Dorothy L. Magnuson's card and recited the address.

"A town outside Portland. We're almost there. He's high-powered, is he?"

"Can you find it?"

Susan asked for a map in the glove box. She laid it across the dashboard and Buckley's lap as she drove. Traffic thickened on a four-laner. Gas stations, junk food, muffler shops, motels, check-cashing outfits, and stop lights every four blocks. Talk about your Third World.

She turned onto a side street, then into a business park a mile and a half from the highway, an array of newish black glass cubes and manicured emerald landscaping. Buckley hazily remembered the area as being trees and pastures, ponds and cows and berry farms, swayback barns, and Burma Shave signs.

Susan asked, "Are you sure he's working today? I don't see many cars."

Buckley scanned a smattering of cars and spotted a silver Mercedes-Benz E320 sedan and its DOTTI vanity plate. Bingo.

"You can drop me here."

"I can wait."

"That's okay," Buckley said, sliding his suitcase out.

Susan noticed the Mercedes. "Your attorney you met on the plane is Dotti?"

"Professionally Dorothy," Buckley said. "Ms. Magnuson."

Susan rolled her eyes.

"Seriously, this is business, Sooz. Hey."

"Hey what?"

"Thanks for hanging on to the Buckley name."

"Buckley's easy to spell. My last husband was Lewendowski. Stop being a stranger to your son and myself, okay?"

"Okay. I promise."

"I know about your promises."

Susan didn't appear too pissed when they said good-bye, but Buckley couldn't believe a vehicle that size was capable of depositing so much rubber on the pavement.

# 5.

Buckley stashed his suitcase in a landscaping display at the front of the complex. Wouldn't do to waltz into a ritzy law office like a hobo. He'd flattened a clump of little blue flowers he hoped would perk up once the luggage was removed.

Buckley watched a uniformed rent-a-cop walk a leisurely patrol in the lobby of Dorothy L. Magnuson's building, an older fella whose gut overlapped his belt buckle.

He waited until the guard was out of sight, then hustled inside and up the stairs. Cline, Sedgwick, Holmes and Magnuson was on the third and top floor. They'd have a swell view if there was anything to see.

Double glass doors thick enough to be bulletproof were locked. Dorothy L. Magnuson and her merry band of lawyers had the sense not to depend on the codger downstairs. She was lettered in gold on a door. Buckley touched her name. The leaf was on the inside, another smart move. There were no lights shining, no sounds. It occurred to him that Dorothy might not necessarily be Dotti. And vice versa.

Buckley wouldn't be able to call a cab from here. Everyone in the world except him owned one of those damn cell phones. He'd have to hoof it to the highway.

He rapped on the door, stinging his tender knuckles, then pounded with the heel of a hand. Dorothy/Dotti came through a corridor holding a file folder. Buckley smiled. She stared.

"On the airplane from Houston," he said.

Dorothy L. Magnuson took a few tentative steps, cupping an ear. Those tentative steps were taken in sandals, toenails unpainted. She wore blue jeans, a Portland Trail Blazers T-shirt and no makeup, a good-looking lady lawyer spending her Sunday shuffling paper.

Buckley repeated himself, louder. No reply. She wasn't giving him a dirty old man look. He'd been down that road. Worse, far worse, she simply didn't recognize him.

"We met on the plane. My son's wedding," he shouted. "I was going to my son's wedding. Out on the beach."

She mouthed "oh" and unlocked the doors. "Yes, of course."

In the reception area, on new-smelling carpeting, her arms folded, Buckley wondering what to do with his hands, he could see she wasn't overjoyed and said, "You said you were also a workaholic like me. I thought I'd take a chance and catch you. I asked if you ever dealt with the government. On the plane."

"Yes. And I said an associate has experience in federal law. He'd have to know the nature of your problem. Antitrust or taxation or something else. I don't know Ron's schedule, but I think he'll in tomorrow."

"I'd rather run it by you first. I don't know Ron. If you have a few minutes."

She said okay, though not exactly clicking her heels, and led him to her private office. Buckley took in the view through picture windows, a golf course of a lawn sloping into a copse of trees, which miraculously hadn't been bulldozed for another business park or a strip mall. There were rows of law books in her bookcase, a good sign.

Wasting no time, Attorney Magnuson sat at a wood slab of a desk piled high with folders and loose paper. Buckley swooshed into a plush leather sofa across from her. Speaking of leather, there was an entire cowhide in that high-backed chair of hers. Classy.

"I saw the Mercedes and the 'Dotti' plate, and put two and two together."

"Dotti's what I go by."

"Nice set of wheels. Spoils of the divorce?"

She narrowed her eyes. "Spoils of being in here on nights and weekends."

His face on fire, Buckley wanted to crawl out through a heating duct. "Can't keep my size ten out of my big friggin' mouth, pardon my French."

Dotti Magnuson broke up. No other way to describe it. She threw up her arms and before long was laughing so hard she was crying. Her nose was running too, and try as she did, she couldn't stop the hysterics. Buckley was afraid she was going to have a seizure. He sprang up, yanked a handful of tissues out of a box on her desk, sending it flying and thrust them at her. She dabbed her eyes and began coughing. Buckley patted her back, as if she were choking on beefsteak, which made her laugh even harder.

She finally recovered. Buckley gave her a clump of tissues. She blew her nose and said, "Sorry, it's not you."

Buckley had the distinct impression it *was* him. He wasn't steamed. He had no right to be, barging in on her like this. Slightly pissed was closer. He made a flourish of looking around. "Don't see anybody else."

Dotti Magnuson leaned forward on her elbows and steepled her fingers. "Okay, indirectly it is you. How you said what you said, you triggered a reaction, and I thank you from the bottom of my heart."

"Yeah. Like a nuclear meltdown reaction."

"Please don't get me going again. I have a sister a year older and one a year younger, stair-step siblings. We had friends in common and held gobs of slumber parties. We'd stay up all night, gossiping, eating popcorn, and braiding each other's hair. Somebody would say something, anything, something totally innocuous, and we'd lose it.

*Completely lose it.* We'd fall into the giggles for half the night. I haven't cut loose like that in years."

Buckley smiled. She'd explained just before all the air escaped from his ego. "Happy to be of service."

"I'm Dotti and you are?"

Buckley nearly spit out Harold (Call Me Hal) Qwerty. Finagle some free hypothetical advice. Compensate her by inviting her out for drinks later.

No, no, no, dammit!

If he was seriously gonna turn his life around and look forward positively, honesty was the best policy. Most of the time.

"Joe. Joe Buckley."

They shook hands. Dotti leaned back in her chair and rocked slightly. "Tell me what Cline Sedgwick can do for you, Joe."

Buckley outlined his pickle. When he finished, he looked at the grandfather clock next to the credenza and said, "My autobiography in ten minutes."

He was sitting straighter, as Dotti had raised her eyebrows in surprise at his age, a silent compliment worth a thousand words.

"Well, you haven't led a dull life. My guess, you being a foreign businessman in Central America, was that you have offshore investment issues. I'm no expert on the UCMJ, the Uniform Code of Military Justice, but I have to wonder if there any specific reason the Army would want you after thirty-plus years. You didn't omit troubles left hanging while you were on active duty?"

"Although I wasn't a model trooper, not soldier of the month material, nope. They don't want me or any deserter per se. They want their pound of flesh. You just flat out don't walk away from Uncle Sam."

"Where was it?" Dotti said, searching her memory. "In a legal journal or the newspaper. Recently, a deserter living in Canada crossed into the U.S. He aroused a Customs agent's professional intuition and they ran him. The military still had an open warrant."

"They forget but they don't forgive," Buckley said. "They never close desertion cases."

"In a court-martial, he was given a bad conduct discharge and sentenced to six months in jail. They reduced it to the one month he spent in the stockade awaiting trial."

"Swell."

"I think it was the Marines. Aren't they much more — what's the term — than the Army?"

"Gung ho. They invented gung ho," Buckley said.

"The Army might be more lenient than the Marine Corps."

Buckley shrugged. "Maybe."

"Joe, isn't your predicament like a root canal? It's not as bad as you make it out to be and you'll feel so much better when it's over."

"That's why I'm here, Dotti," Buckley said, the idea growing on him. "It'll be a relief to have a clean slate. I can come and go on legit ID without looking over my shoulder."

Dotti Magnuson was staring. "Legit as in legitimate?"

Oops, Buckley thought. He smiled sheepishly. "A figure of speech. A complicated story."

"Okay, let's not go there," she said quickly. "I'll talk to Ron when I see him in the morning. I should tell you, if the firm takes a case where the client isn't seeking financial recovery, where we're on a fee, not on a contingency basis, the absolute minimum retainer is three thousand dollars."

Buckley cleared his throat. "Shouldn't be a problem."

Dotti stood. "Great. Can I leave Ron a note saying you'll be calling for an appointment?"

The consultation was over. Buckley stood too. Three thousand smackers. Almost twice as much as his last re-up bonus. An impossible pile of cabbage. He should've known the legal remedy would be too rich for his thinned-out blood and bank account.

"I'll definitely contact Ron. Soon."

"When are you going back to Belize?"

Good question. Buckley thought for a minute, his mind spinning like a compass. "Good question."

"Oh, how was your son's wedding?"

"Wonderful, Dotti. Wonderful."

"And a good time was had by all?"

Not quite realizing he was being shown to the door, Buckley was shown to the door.

"Almost," he said, unconsciously flexing his sore fingers.

"I'm not going there either," she said, observing. "Say, why don't we do this? Write down where you'll be staying and Ron can contact you. As I said, I don't know his schedule."

Buckley dug a wadded cocktail napkin out of a pocket. At an undetermined moment during last night's festivities, Susan had written out her address and phone number, not Seattle, but some little hick burg up by Seattle named Medina.

He gave Dotti the information and took the elevator down.

The plan was this. Hike to the highway, hail a cab to the airport. He flew out tomorrow afternoon. He forgot the departure time; the ticket was in his suitcase. He'd find a cheap motel tonight or curl up in the terminal. He'd slept in worse places and every penny counted.

There'd be no cashing in the airplane ticket, no hanging around for Dotti's Ron. Buckley had a gem of an ex who needed to repair her life, him the hell out of it. His boy had a golden future ahead of him, no thanks to his old man, who had a business to run. And he needed to scram before Harold Roy Qwerty's passport became too warm to the touch.

Buckley did not expect Ron to retain him retainerless, Dotti's recommendation or no recommendation. Sweet as she'd been, he couldn't help being cynical. Less than 50 lawyers were listed in the Belize Yellow Pages. Fifty in the whole country.

Once, Buckley had hoisted a few in a San Ignacio bar with a tipsy tourist out of Kansas City, a lawyer who said his specialty was 1-800-WHIPLASH, just look him up in the Yellow Pages if he ever got to town. The lawyer told him that there were more attorneys in the States than there were people, cats, dogs, chickens and coatimundis in Belize. And they all had to eat.

If Ron did call Susan, she could refer him to Molly's Restaurant, Burns Avenue, San Ignacio, Belize, Central America. If Ron would agree to installment payments, they'd do the deed by remote control. Or not. Him and the United States Army, they'd eventually make their peace. Or not. At least in Belize, if the effort turned to guano, Uncle wouldn't be able to throw a net over him.

Furthermore, Stan seemed to have a notion of him and brother Stan as some sort of criminal museum artifacts. Like Al Capone's Tommy gun. Weird. Buckley intended to do his utmost to narrow the gap between him and his boy. Also best accomplished from long range.

The hefty geezer guard sat on a stool behind a small counter around the corner from the elevator banks, lazing the side of his head against the cool, marble wall, beady eyes tracking Buckley.

"I'm a Cline, Eastwick, Whoever and Magnuson client," Buckley said, and walked outside, unchallenged.

There was a rectangular imprint in the garden bark

where his suitcase had been. The little blue flowers were crushed beyond hope.

This brought two questions to mind:

Who'd want a crummy old suitcase?

What next?

# 6.

In a taxi, staring absently at the back of the driver's turban, Buckley thought that maybe things were working out for the best after all. In that suitcase along with skivvies and shirts was his identity as Joseph J. Buckley. By default he had become either Hal Qwerty of Colorado or nobody. Circumstances were forcing him to live by his wits, maybe even behave responsibly.

On the minus side, he was trapped in the States and low on funds. Any way you sliced it, but for Mr. Qwerty's passport in his back pocket, Joe Buckley was a man without a country.

He took a bus into Portland, laid out more cash than he wanted to at a discount store for toilet articles, clothes and a gym bag to replace the suitcase. He spent the night in the same fleabag, awake longer than asleep.

In the morning he headed north on the Amtrak, running to catch it. Had he missed the train, who knows when he would have reached Seattle? In America, if you didn't own a car you were basically screwed and stranded wherever you were. That hadn't changed over the years.

Buckley tended to rationalize a circuitous path through life, a fact apparent to anyone close to him and occasionally to himself. Thanks to a chronic haplessness, he hadn't completely lost his innocence.

He concluded that he should pop in on Susan, see whether he really could smooth over the spat between her and Andrew. Apologize to the aspiring, genius artist, kiss his ass, do whatever he had to do. While there, try to establish rapport with his son. And definitely work out an easy payment plan with Dotti's lawyer colleague, Ron.

Be proactive. That's what he'd be, proactive. He had heard the word on CNN. You were proactive, you turned your life around. You were proactive, the fickle finger of fate ceased being a proctologist's digit.

"Are you sure you know where you're going? I swear we backtracked a couple of times."

"Yes sir," said the cab driver Buckley had hailed at the Seattle Amtrak station.

"The meter runs much longer, you'll own me, pal. Medina is a flyspeck on the map. Sure we haven't gone by it?"

"No sir. Medina, while small, is a notable enclave of the relatively-old rich and the newly affluent."

He talked like a British officer out of an old Khyber Pass flick. "No fooling?"

Susan's little town was a Seattle suburb on Lake Washington, a large body of water east of the city. Seattle had grown by leaps and bounds since he'd visited when stationed at Fort Lewis. He wasn't quite sure where he was and didn't remember two bridges spanning the lake then.

They'd seen the Medina signs, yeah, but Susan's town was a non-town. There were few businesses on this road that might or might not be the main drag and fewer visible residences. The lakeside was mostly trees and hedges as tall and long and flat as an aircraft carrier, and iron fences. A swanky neighborhood. Buckley wondered whether there was that much money in fender bending, whether Susan had taken the body and paint man to the cleaners, although she wasn't the type.

"Hey, we've been by that mailbox," Buckley said. "That's where I get out."

"I do not believe so, sir."

"Well, I do. Stop!"

The driver obeyed, throwing Buckley against the front

seat.

He rubbed his chest. If he told Susan, he'd get another seat belt lecture. He paid the cabby, who told him to have a splendid day.

Buckley checked the mailbox. Wrong box. He walked a quarter mile to the right one. No name on it, but the street number matched.

There was a gate for cars, and a button and speaker. The people gate was locked, although a sloppy fit. Buckley reached through the bars and depressed the bolt with his comb. Some security.

Buckley walked down a sloping flagstone driveway, a fishing road without the ruts. Trees crowded each side, small and neat and uniform, like spectators at a race. A rufous-sided towhee scuttled through fallen leaves amongst them. Bird species 290 on his life list.

Towhees looked like robins; you had to know your birds. He'd probably seen thousands of towhees growing up, when a bird was just a bird.

He came to a clearing. Sprinklers fizzed in great arcs, keeping the lawn as green as Dotti's business park's. Gardeners trimmed shrubs and weeded flowerbeds. They paid Buckley no attention as he continued toward a tall, detached garage. He counted the doors: nine. An apartment or condo complex, he decided, and not in the budget category.

Buckley went around a side and his jaw dropped. The lake was spread out before him, flat and glossy and dotted with boats. This property sported a dock and a boat tied up that was bigger than the water taxis that ran between Belize City and the cays. On the Seattle side, tops of skyscrapers spiked up from behind hills.

To the right of the garage, beyond a patio the size of a parking lot was a house, if you could call it that. A series of hammerheaded cubes, both stacked and overlapping, poked out of the ground like a clump of square toadstools. The conglomeration was stuccoed and red tile roofed and glass galore. Decks extended hither and yon from the floor-to-ceiling windows.

"Holy cow!"

Gaping, Buckley stumbled on a low step and almost fell into the swimming pool. He scrambled to his knees and clutched at a chaise lounge that splashed in instead. He pulled it out and held it up to drip dry, puzzled why you needed a pool if you were on a lake or, vice versa, why you needed to live on a lake when you could afford a pool.

"Look what the cat dragged in."

Susan was standing in a doorway, wearing shades and a housecoat decorated like an arboretum, hands on hips. Buckley knew that posture well.

"Oh, hi, Sooz."

"I know, you just happened to be in the neighborhood."

Was she the maid? He dropped the lounge and settled in another. "As a matter of fact. You said don't be a stranger."

She dragged a chair across from him sat. "Words that will haunt me. Did you and your lawyer make progress?"

"Absolutely. She's taking my case and thinks I have a good chance of leniency. It's been assigned to another lawyer in the office who's an expert in dealing with Uncle Sam. My situation is looking up. Since I have to hang around, I thought I'd see if I could, as I offered, patch things up with Andrew. For your sake. Apologize to him." Buckley tapped his nose. "Let him take a free poke at me if he so desires."

"That's sweet, Joe, but is there something you're not telling me?"

Buckley frowned. "Like what?"

"Like anything. You have that look."

"What look?"

"Oh, the look you had when you lost your bar tips to that waiter, I forget his name, shooting craps on the pool table after closing. I was six months along with Stanley, thinking we could use the money. Silly me. I have other examples."

"What you have is the memory of an elephant. I don't know what you mean by that look and I don't gamble any more. Let's just say fate brought me up here to do the right thing. See my boy too. We didn't have much of a chance at the wedding, him and me."

"They're on their honeymoon."

"I'll miss him?"

"It'll be a short trip. They went up to British Columbia. Stanley has obligations coming out of his ears."

Buckley slapped his hands together. "So where's Andrew? Invite him over or take me to him so I can get that show on the road."

"Impossible."

"You've seen him, talked to him?"

"Yes."

"Okay, what's wrong?"

She took off the sunglasses and dabbed red eyes with a hankie. "He's gone, moved out."

"You lived here, you and *him*?"

"Yes, Joe, in sin." She pointed at the garage. "We lived above, in the coach house. When I got home, Andrew had cleared out. And you know what else? He took my diaries too. I called and asked for them. He hung up on me all three times."

Her voice was cracking. Buckley slid his lounge next to her. "You gotta have a library's worth of those babies by now."

"A box full. It was always a bone of contention that I refused to let him read them."

"I didn't once ask or try to sneak a peek, Sooz."

Susan patted his arm. "I know, Joe. You're my only husband who didn't. Have I ever mentioned Mike?"

"Nope. A husband I missed?"

"Don't be a smart-ass. Mike and I were engaged. He was a locksmith. The teensy locks on the diaries were child's play. I suspected he'd been into them. They were out of order on the shelf. I asked, he denied. I didn't believe him and stuck a hair between pages. You know, like spies do in a doorjamb to learn if they'd had company. Sure enough, no hair. I confronted Mike. He went into a huff and said if I didn't trust him we had no future. I said I agreed. I don't know if it was my lurid past or purplish prose that kept him turning the pages."

Buckley couldn't help but laugh.

"In retrospect, Andrew is incredibly insecure, a side of him I hadn't previously experienced."

"That's grand larceny," Buckley said, shaking his head. "I'm no one to talk, but what he is is a goddamn felon."

"Andrew has a loft in Seattle. I'll give him a day to cool off, then go over and try to reason with him about the diaries and the rest."

"Are they incriminating?"

"Only my life story. You were a feature attraction in the earlier books."

"Uh huh. Starring as Snidely Whiplash. How'd you ever hook up with Andrew?"

"I took a course in art appreciation from him at community college. The rest is history."

"That's nice that you can get time off to take care of stuff like this."

"Time off from what?" Susan said.

Buckley scanned the property, swiveling his head a good forty-five degrees each way to take it all in. "Whose cozy bungalow is this?"

"Stanley's. Whose did you think it was?"

Buckley whistled. "You never said."

"You never asked. I've been living with Stanley six months now, since the home was completed."

"This little hick town, Medina, I've never heard of it."

Susan laughed. "The per capita income of this little hick town probably exceeds Beverly Hills's."

"Yeah. Looks like it's got the gross national product of God."

"Well put."

"I knew he was doing okay." Buckley couldn't continue.

"Stanley is doing fabulously okay. He is founder and CEO of sjbWare."

"I know that."

"You don't seem to comprehend, Joe. Their principal product, sjbBoost, dominates its market. Stanley got in on the ground floor. Boost is installed in four out of five PC's that roll off the assembly line and the company has divisions that are making inroads in the server and mainframe markets, as well as overseas."

"Smart boy we produced, Sooz."

"I should say so. sjbWare grossed a billion dollars last year."

"Billion, B as in bucks, as in Daddy Warbucks?"

Susan nodded. "*Billion.*"

"Why the small letters? Me, I'd have the SJB in flashing neon."

"Because understatement jumps off the page, Stanley feels. My theory, just between you and I, is subconscious modesty and shyness. Stanley always was bashful and introspective."

"That pad at Cannon Beach, it wasn't a rental for the wedding, huh?"

"Goodness, no. It's his. Theirs."

Buckley was speechless.

"Joe, you're measuring success in the context of you or me or an average person getting ahead. A raise and a move to a split-level and a minivan to take the kiddies to Disneyland. Stanley is on an entirely different scale. sjb's stock value exceeds the annual budget of some nations."

"His wife works for him, you said."

"Knowing Beth, in some respects it'll be the other way around if he isn't careful. Beth does fine in her own right. I'll give her that. She's as smart as he is and works just as hard. While not in Stanley's league, she's a millionaire on stock options."

"She's not a gold digger?"

"No. She didn't marry him for his money, I'm convinced."

"Beth's gonna stay home, stay barefoot and pregnant?"

"Please. You know, you're stuck in a 1965 time warp. Should bambinos be in the scenario, Stanley might have to carry them."

"I thought computer stocks went in the crapper. They blew tons of borrowed money and didn't make a red cent. Whadduya call it, burn rate."

"sjbWare took a hit too, but rebounded. They have a business plan and made money from day one. sjbWare isn't a silly little dot-com. Stanley cashed in stock when it was still sky high to build here. He barely felt the downturn. He razed an early-forties house, as well as the houses on the adjacent lots he bought too, to triple the land."

"We're early-forties vintage too, kiddo," Buckley said.

"It's what these software people do. Bill Gates is a neighbor."

Jesus H. Christ, Buckley thought. My son the kazillionaire.

"The kids will be back from Canada toward the middle

of the week. Movers should be here later today or tomorrow moving Beth in, Irene supervising, naturally."

"Our boy wasn't living in sin, huh?" Buckley said.

"No. He's no chip off the old Buckley block. Besides, Irene would've had a cow."

Buckley swept a hand. "Their love nest is, uh, different."

"They are living in their notion of architectural paradise. The Cannon Beach cabin wasn't a Dolley Madison dream home out of personal preference. Twenty-seventh Century Gothic wouldn't fly past the zoning board.

"Stanley, bless him, is a dyed-in-the-wool nerd. If he or Beth picks up a novel, it's sci-fi or fantasy. This pad may be straight from a space opera set in the Alpha Centauri system. Stanley, remember, is opaque.

"You want to spit it out, Buckley?"

"Spit what out?"

"Any idiot can see that you have a five-hundred-pound albatross chained around your neck."

Buckley spit out the purloined suitcase story.

"Good grief, Joe."

"Any way you slice it, I'm a man without a country."

"Your lady friend's Ron might be able to straighten out your ID mess too."

"Maybe, given enough time and money."

"Can you pay the retainer?"

"No sweat."

"Joe."

"I'll work out an easy payment plan with them."

"I could help."

Buckley shook his head. "I've never taken advantage of a woman. For money."

"I'm glad you qualified that. These little imbroglios of yours could be solved out of petty, petty cash. If you won't take money from me, Stanley would be happy to help out."

Imbroglios.

"Not a chance. I'm plenty of things. Moocher ain't one of them. I took five cents from him, I wouldn't be able to face myself in a mirror."

"Like Sinatra, you're doing it your way. I admire your boneheaded pride to a point. I suppose you can stay here, at least until the kids get back from that excuse of a honeymoon. You should have time to find out where you stand legally. You wouldn't be a charity case. You wouldn't be costing us anything except food and beer in the fridge."

Buckley cocked his head at the square mushrooms. "I couldn't just move in on them. Uh uh."

"I meant the coach house."

He smiled. "In the coach house where you are?"

"Don't get any ideas, Buckley. You'll have one wing, I have mine."

Buckley shrugged. "I appreciate your hospitality, Sooz. I sincerely do."

"Another condition."

"Sure."

"If Andrew and I kiss and make up, I'll notify you *immediately*. I'll expect every single trace of you gone lickety-split. I mean it. Forget about making nicey-nice with him. I don't think it would take and you here, physically here with me, he'd go ballistic, not that I could blame him."

"Can do."

"*Will* do, that is the question."

"You know me, Sooz."

"That's the trouble. I do know you"

# 7.

After two days rattling around above his son's garage and roaming the grounds, Buckley didn't know the official medical term, but he definitely had a dose of Backasswards Claustrophobia.

In San Ignacio, in Mrs. Castanada's rooming house, Buckley shared the second floor bathroom and an outdoor storage shed. He had few belongings and knew where everything was in his cubbyhole.

His boy's place, inside and out, for Chrissake, was the wide-open spaces.

His wing of Susan's coach house consisted of a full kitchen stocked with food and drink, bedroom, bath, living room and fireplace. Aside from a bed, a table and chairs, and a sofa, there was no furniture. All that hardwood flooring and carpet made Buckley think if you flooded and froze it, you could play hockey.

A cold snap had given him ice on the brain. In Belize you never saw any that wasn't in a glass. When it became certain that the afternoon temperature had stalled at 65°, Buckley started a fire.

Lightweight jacket zippered, Buckley kicked back by a picture window facing the water. His craving for current reading matter hadn't diminished. Before newspapers went into the fire with the kindling and green firewood, Buckley read every page, including the slippery, brassy advertising inserts. Cellular phones, rib steaks, recliner chairs, fall school clothes. The unending variety and hot color was pure magic.

There were paperback romance novels in the firewood

box too, Susan's. Buckley thought of them as discarded candy wrappers.

He opened one at random and read, "High voltage electricity crackled between them. His powerful hands clasped Clarisse's waist, drawing her to him. She felt the rocklike muscles of his legs. Her head fell back, lips parted helplessly to receive his kiss. Unstoppable desire surged through her loins as he hungrily explored her pulsating womanhood."

Buckley assumed the sport taking the direct approach was the pirate on the cover. He tossed the book in the fire. The writing wasn't hot enough to give a fella a boner. What it did for gals, he couldn't imagine. His 60 years might not have been such a bumpy road if he'd understood women just a little bit.

Susan's wing was at least as large, not that he'd ever see the inside. Killjoy that she was, Sooz was serious about no hanky-panky and kept her door bolted. There was a common entry area above the stairs. A framed canvas hung on the wall opposite the door.

Susan had noticed Buckley noticing and asked, "What do you think?"

It looked like potato salad on a bed of Popsicle-blue lettuce. Buckley rubbed his chin and frowned, stalling.

"Andrew's", Susan told him. "It's entitled *The View from Trieste*."

He'd heard of Trieste. It was a city or country somewhere. This thing was Hiroshima or Nagasaki. He visualized a room full of Andrew's pictures as a boiler explosion in a paint store.

"Uh huh. Right. Pretty."

The critique earned him a slammed door.

Susan hadn't been around much. She didn't confide her activities, but he knew she was trying her damnedest to make up with Andrew. He'd lie awake, hear her coming in, closing doors, and then he'd finally nod off. She had not spent an entire night in the artist loft.

Buckley had explored the garage, amazed. Bright fluorescent lights, shelving holding stuff stored just so, a painted floor you could eat off of. That monster SUV was out, evidently Susan's favorite. There was a bechromed Jeep on waist-high knobby tires, made for the off-road, but showroom shiny. Next to it an empty stall, probably reserved for whatever Stan and his bride took up to Canada. Two convertibles also, a new 3-series Beemer and a vintage Mercedes, which flanked a massive Mercedes S-Class. Good luck driving the ragtops in Seattle's Arctic climate.

The last car made Buckley drool, a '58 or '59 Chevy Corvette, slung low in black and silver, three carbs and four on the floor. An automotive wet dream when Buckley was a kid, the Vette still looked fast. It'd haul ass. Dave Kenworthy, his best Army buddy, had spent his re-up bonus on the same, except Dave's was red and white.

He wondered what had happened to the Schwinn. It'd be puny and trashy in comparison. They could store it in the attic. If they had an attic instead of a coach house. He supposed it was already in a landfill.

Earlier, Buckley had found a pair of binoculars on a shelf and walked out to the end of the dock. He didn't know anything about boats other than Stan's was a big, tall, wide, long, new-looking cabin cruiser. It bobbed there, tied up, forlorn and neglected. It didn't even have a name. Maybe Stan owned it because you oughta have a boat tied up at your dock like your neighbors, who all did. When you were rich beyond rich, you had to shell out for appearance. It was expected.

Buckley wiped the dust off the glasses and had the first fun he'd had lately. A great blue heron on a stump, a living statue. A V-formation of Canada geese flapped overhead, like B-17's headed for Nazi Germany. He swept the shoreline: American coots, mallards, hooded mergansers, red-winged blackbirds, western gulls, buffleheads and a goldeneye. A red-tailed hawk circled inland, corkscrewing downward, a doomed rodent in its sights. A bald eagle atop a snag made Buckley's day.

The merganser, coot and goldeneye rang his life list up to 293. A few more temperate region birds that didn't migrate as far south as Belize and he'd be over the 300 hurdle.

He should be phoning Dotti's Ron, setting something up. The ideal approach would be to go down there in person and lay out the situation. Once Buckley mulled it, he decided being in the country without identification wasn't necessarily a problem. He was, after all, an American citizen.

Theoretically, he wasn't in the U.S. illegally if he'd never left in the first place. His 18 years in Belize was a technicality that didn't exist if he didn't raise the subject or try to cross a border. Handled properly, the beef with the Army would be his only hassle.

Susan had been coming and going in shorter interims. She'd briefly stop in on Buckley, ask how it was going, and he'd say fine. He'd ask how it was going and she'd say fine. He figured she had some sort of shuttle diplomacy in motion with Andrew. She didn't seem happy enough to indicate there'd been progress on the forgiveness front. The diaries might be the hang-up. To the best of his knowledge, she hadn't brought any home.

Just Philip was another possibility. Buckley had been a steady customer for so long, his credit ought to be good. Give Just Philip a jingle, talk over his pickle, see what he could do, settle up later. If he were careful, his remaining cash would cover airfare and that obligation.

Beeline for home. That made the most sense. He did

have a business to run.

Or just go with the flow for the moment, Buckley thought, opening another cold brew. Hang around, see his boy, let the chips fall as they may.

A moving truck arrived, closely followed by mother-in-law Irene in a gray Honda sedan. Buckley watched her supervise what appeared to be a pair of college kids. These were people who could afford any moving van company on the planet. What was that new yuppie word he saw on a TV program? Micromanage, that was it.

After his beer was gone, he went over to say hello, not to mention to sneak a peek inside Stan's mansion.

Irene stood in a doorway, holding a clipboard, calling instructions in to the workers. There were piles of luggage and wedding presents (no Schwinn) and furniture. Buckley said hello.

Irene looked at him and asked, "Are you the chief caretaker?"

She didn't recognize him. There was an epidemic of that going around. The good news was that she'd obviously departed the wedding festivities before him and Andrew locked antlers.

Up close and personal, Irene was maybe five years younger than Buckley, a moonfaced, blandly semi-attractive lady whose features you'd forget five minutes out of her sight. Her crow's feet registered, however. They'd been etched in deeply, as if someone had used a straightedge and a razor blade.

Buckley evaded the question by pointing at the presents. "They really cleaned up, huh?"

"Have you seen the housekeeper today?"

Not today or any other day. "Nope."

"When you do, would you please mention linens and towels? And inform your people that the juniper along the north side is taking over the flower beds."

"Linens and towels," Buckley said. "Prune the juniper. Gotcha. Yes ma'am."

"Linen in the master suite appears fresh, but I'm not absolutely positive, and they will be returning tomorrow."

"Tomorrow?"

"Work obligations," Irene said. "They're abbreviating the honeymoon."

"That's a shame," Buckley said.

"In retrospect, honeymoons aren't what they're cracked up to be," Irene said.

Buckley didn't reply. He wasn't gonna touch that one with this tense, unfriendly lady. We're talking live grenade here, he thought.

"You'll check?"

"Yes ma'am. You betcha," Buckley said. "Linens and towels and juniper."

"I don't mean to tell you how to do your job," Irene said. "I find it best to write everything down. Goodness knows, my memory isn't what it used to be."

"Likewise, ma'am," Buckley said, writing on a scrap of paper in his pants pocket.

He went back to his coach house wing. A breeze was whipping up, nose-diving the wind-chill factor into the upper fifties.

Not so long ago, Buckley would've jumped through hoops to get into Irene's knickers, just for the sheer challenge. Older and somewhat wiser, Buckley realized it'd be like climbing Everest, except without the glory. The summit would amount to bitter cold. A dumb, pointless, egotistical seduction that'd do nothing for either party.

Buckley fed his scribbled instructions into the dying fire and got a fresh beer. Susan returned and knocked on his door.

She came in, fanning herself, asking him if he'd gone crazy.

"Your blood isn't as thin as broth," he said, rubbing his palms together over the smoldering flames.

Her eyes were redder than they'd been when she sprang the news that Andrew moved out. She was dolled up, in a nice red dress, tight but not overly tight as befitting a lady of her years. Radioactive blue eye shadow, silver hair stacked up to the heavens and sprayed into position, high-octane perfume, the full nine yards.

She fanned herself again, opened a window without asking permission, went to the fridge for a beer, sat across from Buckley, popped the top, and said, "Oh boy."

Meaning Andrew. Another subject Buckley wasn't touching with a 10-foot pole. He waited.

"He's gone," she said.

"Andrew?

"Andrew."

"Gone where?"

"To L.A."

"Los Angeles? Andrew moved to La La Land?"

"I don't know if it's permanent or a visit. One of the other artists who has a studio in the building said he packed up *fast* and headed to the airport. His unit is locked and I don't have a key. I gave mine back to him when we moved in here."

"Maybe it's a family emergency," said a helpful Buckley. "They're always sudden."

"He's estranged from his family," Susan said. "Sudden is right on the mark. He almost knocked another artist down on the steps with his suitcase."

"So there you go," Buckley said. "A suitcase. He didn't take his pictures. He'll be back."

"Paintings. We had a date. I truly believed we were over most of the hurdles."

"Sorry."

"Thanks, Joe, but he could have, should have called

me if he was running out. I hurt him, so he set me up to be hurt. He knows the diaries are raw nerves. Wherever they are. I should have my head examined. I was Peggy Guggenheim to his Jackson Pollock."

"Sooz, you wanna translate that into English?"

She sighed. "I was his benefactor, his patron. He loved what I could do for him financially and to advance his career. Period."

Buckley suspected as much. Andrew, the rancid son of a bitch. "Not a chance, Sooz. You're too damn lovable."

"You are the world's sweetest liar."

"We could break in, in case he left the diaries behind. Go in tonight after dark. My brother Stan taught me a couple of burglary tricks I haven't forgotten."

Susan smiled and shook her head wearily.

"Well, listen, Sooz, we could go out to dinner or whatever. Strictly companionship, you know."

"Thanks for the offer. You're a doll. I'll hang loose. You could be right. An emergency Andrew didn't have time to notify me about."

"By the way, the newlyweds will be back tomorrow."

"You talked to them?"

"Irene told me. She's moving Beth in."

Susan's eyes widened. "You and Irene?"

"Trust me, the conversation was brief and totally innocent."

"Did she say why?"

"Only that honeymoons aren't what they're cracked up to be."

"Like daughter, like mother? I sincerely hope not. You and I didn't have a honeymoon."

"Nope. Not if you don't count beforehand. Somebody'd quit in the kitchen and the bar on the day on the wedding."

Susan said, "I remember. We were working at the Come-On-Inn Restaurant and Lounge, south of Tacoma, out past Parkland. Half the clientele were GI's from Fort Lewis and McChord Air Force Base, half locals."

Buckley shuddered at the memory. "Locals and GIs. Like mixing oil and water."

"When we worked the bar, you probably broke up a fight a night."

"Those were the days," Buckley said. "I'd wade in with a baseball bat in one hand, a seltzer bottle in the other. We had to report for our shifts that afternoon or be canned. We stowed your wedding dress and veil in the car."

"Memories," Susan said, showing her age as she slowly got up.

"By the way again, how'd you find me in San Ignacio? Hire a detective?"

"That's for me to know and you to find out. I'll be in my room crying and/or throwing things."

Buckley gazed out at the lake. The powered boats and the sailboats were on the move, a good 80 percent of them. They couldn't just sit there. They were going somewhere, doing something. The if-we-can-put-man-on-the-moon mentality. Eighteen years in exile and he did not for a single day miss the American can-do mentality.

The three of four Belizeans who didn't live in Belize City swore they never would, not because of congestion or pollution or crime or hurricanes, but because of the "fast pace". There weren't five traffic lights in the entire town. If they wanted fast pace, thought the homesick Buckley, they oughta be up north, watching folks relax on this lake.

He heard a car door slam. He looked down at what he knew in his younger days as a bubble gum machine. Red glass domes on the roofs of 1957 Fords had been superseded by multicolored light bars. This one was blue and red and clear, and it was no consolation that it wasn't flashing. A uniformed cop stood directly below, rapping on the door.

Shit, Buckley thought. Andrew ratted him out before skedaddling to La La Land. Buckley went downstairs to face the music. If it had to happen, better now than tomorrow. He'd hate to have his boy see him packed off in cuffs.

From the station house, he'd use his one phone call to contact Dotti and/or Ron, although he wasn't certain how his easy payment proposition would fly. That failing, they could refer him to a public defender.

He'd take his medicine like a man. Providing he survived prison, he'd skulk on home to Belize.

"Good afternoon, sir," the cop said politely. "Is this your residence?"

He was even younger than Stan. "I'm a guest."

"From out of town?"

Here it comes. "Uh, yeah. Yes sir."

"I don't know if you're aware that there's a burn ban in effect for air quality purposes. Your chimney smoke was reported. I'm afraid I'll have to ask you to extinguish the fire."

"No sweat," said a relieved Buckley, grinning idiotically. "Can do."

# 8.

The honeymooners returned not tomorrow, but six o'clock that very evening. Respiration and heartbeat approaching normal after his scrape with the law, Joe Buckley observed them unloading a Volvo station wagon, thinking the honeymoon might've lasted a lot longer had they taken the Corvette, adrenaline and hormones pumping on the open road.

Susan greeted them with hugs that Beth sideslipped and Stan accepted good-naturedly, then assisted with the luggage. She waved furiously at Buckley to come on down.

Stan wore khaki slacks and a blue shirt. Eyes surprised behind smudged glasses, he shook Buckley's hand. "Good to see you again."

"You too," he told his son.

Beth smiled tightly and said hello. She also wore khaki shorts and a blue blouse. Her hair was brushed and her glasses weren't smudged. Otherwise, they could be twins, dressed by their parents for a picnic.

She was entitled to be testy, him making himself at home. They both were.

Buckley reciprocated the polite hello. He wasn't about to ask how the honeymoon trip went, a loaded question if there ever was one.

"Joe was able to squeeze in a few more days," Susan said.

"How nice," Beth said.

"Let's hope his restaurant survives without him," Susan said.

"Let's hope," Beth said, screwing the smile even

tighter.

"Uh huh," Stan said, wrestling the Schwinn out of the Volvo.

That Buckley was touched was an understatement. "Take it for a spin?"

"I was planning to," Stan said vaguely.

Irene pulled into the driveway in her gloomy-colored Honda.

Taking a hint, Buckley said, "Actually, I have a plane to catch. You know how running a business is. Blink your eyes and it'll fall apart on you."

"Joe," Susan said.

"I'll say good-bye on my way out."

Buckley went upstairs, thinking how stupid he'd been to come here. He'd been out of their lives so long, he wasn't a stranger, he was an intruder. Traveling lighter than light, it took him ninety seconds to pack the gym bag.

Susan blocked the door.

Typical," she said. "Typical Joe Buckley. When you're a little uncomfortable, you scram."

Story of my life. If you wanna be helpful, Sooz, you can call me a cab."

"Okay, you're a cab."

"Hilarious. Listen, in this situation, five's a crowd."

"Beth and Irene are none too keen on my presence either. That's no excuse to fly into a panic."

"Is Beth gonna evict you?"

Susan rolled her eyes. "Since I'm no longer living in sin with Andrew, I think she's made peace with my existence. I've been looking for my own place too. Where're you going?"

"Portland, to that lawyer. I need to move on my problem. As is, I'm pretty much screwed. Earlier, someone complained about the fireplace smoke. A cop came to the door and I liked to of peed my pants. I need to flush the paranoia out of my system, head to my comfort zone before I gotta be fitted for adult diapers. Even if it means doing the responsible thing."

"Stay up here for five full minutes. I'll take care of your cab," Susan said.

Buckley obliged, enjoying a final look at the lake. He walked out to see Stan behind the wheel of the Corvette, top down, revving it up, belching blackish smoke out of dual exhausts.

Susan was leaning on the driver's door. She pecked his cheek and said, "Stanley will drive you to the airport. Buckley, once again, don't be a stranger."

Susan playing a father-son version of Cupid, bless her heart. No sign of Beth and Irene, though conversation and carelessly handled objects reverberated from inside.

Buckley got into the car. "Hey, swell, but I don't want to put you out, you know, just getting in from Canada."

"Not a problem," Stan said, fiddling with the shifter. "Mom suggested I give the car a romp. It sits too long."

"Yeah, burn out the carbon. You gotta do it with these golden oldies," Buckley said inanely. "Good policy."

Stan wasn't making eye contact. Buckley couldn't guess whether Susan had wheedled him into the gesture or Beth had also put a bug in his ear, saying get rid of the old bastard, or the boy simply jumped on an excuse to drive the Vette. Opaque that he was. Grateful in any case for the end result, Buckley naturally preferred the last.

"I really appreciate this," Buckley said, a mile from the mansion, breaking the silence.

"As I said, it does sit too long at a stretch. We're doing the car's drivetrain a favor."

"Blowing out the carbon. You gotta blow out the carbon," Buckley said, speaking up to be heard over the engine and slipstream. He'd forgotten how loud these old babies were and forgotten how chilled he ought to be now.

"A good buddy of mine in the service named Dave Kenworthy had a Vette, about the same year as yours, but his was red and white."

Stan nodded.

"He was always tinkering under the hood, to keep it running smooth. Tri-power, you know, three four-barrel carbs, it was an art to keep them synchronized, kind of like tuning a piano. Dave tuned by ear. No machines."

"Yes," Stan said. "This car's in the shop continually. Everything's fuel injection nowadays and nobody now knows multi-carburetion. Your buddy, was he in the department that fixed motor vehicles?"

"Motor pool."

"That's it."

"Nah. That was too logical for the Army. They made Dave into a cook too. We were stationed at Fort Bliss together, in Texas, down by the border. We drove all over Texas in his Vette. Ran like a top. Dave was a good guy, one of my best friends ever. He was killed in Vietnam."

"A cook killed in combat?"

"They lobbed mortar rounds into the mess tent, figuring they'd get a whole bunch of troops. These were US-made 81-millimeter shells we'd given to the South Vietnamese that Charlie had helped himself to. That or our allies sold them out the back door to them.

"GI's bitch nonstop about the chow, but you know what, they seldom miss a meal and the guys who bitch the loudest are usually at the head of the chow line. The VC got their wires crossed. They hit them between meals, so they only nailed Dave and the mess sergeant and a couple of Vietnamese civilian KP's and a civet cat the cooks had caught and tamed that lived on leftovers."

"That was after you were there?"

"No, actually before, early in the war when GI casualties were relatively uncommon. Dave was in the wrong place at the wrong time."

"What was Vietnam like for you?"

"I was there fairly early too. I rotated home just before the built-up went full tilt. It was like gravy stateside duty. I cooked at a Tan Son Nhut mess hall for twelve months and got fifty-five bucks a month extra combat pay. Tan Son Nhut was the huge airbase outside of Saigon."

"Did you see any action?"

"Not of the John Wayne variety. It was a goofy period in history. We believed in why we were there and had no doubt that we'd win, no matter how screwed up things were. It's been years and years. The fine details are fuzzy, especially anything bad. I survived, didn't get a scratch."

"May I ask you a question?"

By the way the boy asked if he could ask, butterflies launched in Buckley's stomach. "Okay, sure."

"You'd been in the service a while, right?"

"Right."

"You had your Vietnam tour behind you."

"Right."

"So why did you desert?"

"Your mother told you, huh?"

"No, Andrew did."

"He did, she didn't?"

"Correct. She had said that you lived out of the country. I'd ask why. She'd go, he has his reasons, whatever they are."

Buckley felt like a jerk thinking for an instant that Susan had badmouthed his fugitive old man to him. "I was young. I pulled plenty of bonehead stunts and that one took the cake."

They were on a Lake Washington floating bridge. The water was glassy on one side, choppy on the other. Traffic was as thick as sludge in each direction, more cars on the bridge deck, Buckley gauged, than registered in all of Cayo

District, of which San Ignacio was the capital. Buckley noticed a red-tailed hawk perched on a light standard, waiting for supper to come along. In Belize, the roadside hawk was a common species, but he'd seen nary a red-tail.

Buckley cleared his throat and said, "Anyhow, I felt like quitting the Army, so that's what I did. It's a headache I realize I should of rectified by now."

Looking out at the water, he paused and shrugged. "But I haven't."

Then Joe Buckley blurted, "I don't blame you for hating me."

"I don't hate you."

"That's what your mother said too. It's understandable if you do."

"You're not the only father who shirked his responsibilities. You're not a statistical anomaly. I don't honestly feel I've suffered long-term. None of my temporary stepfathers were bad people. If they were, Mom suppressed their negative traits, at least as far as their behavior impacted me. By and large, they were adequate."

Buckley digested that quietly. He should have been relieved, but wasn't. The boy was so cool, so detached. He almost preferred an outburst of tears and cuss words, Stan getting it out in the open, screaming that his biological old man was a rancid piece-of-shit, et cetera.

"You and Andrew and Mom at the wedding, may I address that issue?"

Buckley took a deep breath. "Fire away."

"Beth and I had left. My mother-in-law too, thankfully. We heard stories later. I have to tell you, it grossed people out. Beth and Irene, they're torqued over it, big time."

"One thing led to another. I apologize."

"I'm not necessarily blaming you. Andrew was being a jerk, his normal functioning mode."

"I made it easy for him. I did not discourage him. I

tend not to discourage guys who wanna take a swing, like I should. At my age."

"Mom said you liked to mix it up when you were younger. Sorry, I just had to bring it up."

"That's okay and it's basically water under the bridge except for an exception now and again." Buckley stroked his ruined nose and smiled. "A misspent youth. I'd fly off the handle at the drop of a hat. I see the evidence every morning when I shave."

Stan looked at him. "Was Uncle Stan scarred too? I can't tell from the photos."

"Nope. Stan was a far superior fighter than me. When he got going, his fists were a blur. It was the other guy who ended up eating through a straw."

"Really? He was that good?"

"He was good at stuff that led him to an early death."

"Between you and me, I never much cared for Andrew. I think he was a fortune hunter using Mom to further his career. If their breakup is permanent, it was worth the disruption. I was scared to death she'd marry him."

"He pushed and shoved me first. Letting the other guy have the first punch, it's against my policy. You should never let the other guy have the first punch if you know he's gonna," Buckley explained, massaging his nearly healed knuckles. "I coldcocked him out of respect for the names he called your mother and out of instinct. I am real sorry. I shouldn't of let my temper fly out of control at such a special occasion."

"Forget it." Stan said. "Tell me about my namesake, my Uncle Stan."

*Uncle* Stan. Buckley was increasingly jealous of his dead, worthless brother.

"He was the black sheep of the family. The blackest of us two sheep, that is."

They were across the lake, in a tunnel, taillights

furiously blinking in the stop and go. Stan Buckley laughed at his black sheep remark, startling his father. It was a chuckling sound, an engine turning over, but unwilling to start.

"We were wild kids and I gotta tell you, the Army, for its faults, probably saved my life. Stan got hauled before the same judge as me, for stealing hubcaps or some other penny ante offense. If you were at loose ends, bound to come to no good on the path you were on, this judge gave you the choice of the recruiting station or the pokey. They could do that back then. Stan lost the chance to choose by smart-mouthing Hissonor. He did six months on a county farm and acquired friends even nastier than ones he already had.

"He came out thinking robbing banks was easy money. Maybe it was for folks like Bonnie and Clyde, but Stan never perfected the technique. His last bank was when they'd started using dye packs and the branches were being outfitted with silent alarms where the tellers could step on a button. Stan hadn't kept current on the advances."

Stan said, "Technology passing people by. I see it every day."

"Yeah. That's why I'm gonna make my restaurant into a cybercafé. Anyways, they were waiting for Stan outside the bank, an army of cops. This bag of loot they gave him exploded in a cloud of dye. Stan must've looked like the Pink Panther. I'm unclear whether he had a gun or made a threatening move that made them think he did. I know he was desperate. He had no particular interest in an encore at Salem, which is where the Oregon State Pen is."

"Shot down on the street like John Dillinger," Stan said, shaking his head.

"He was my brother, and I loved him strictly for that alone, but he asked for it," Buckley replied, in a voice that lowered a fraction of an octave, resonating with an unfamiliar fatherliness. "In my heart, I needed to honor his memory, although he was a no-good, worthless bum. We weren't close as tots or as adults. I gotta let you know, I'm incredibly proud of how you turned out, breaking the Buckley mold."

"You and Mom had a dispute over naming me, ending in a compromise."

"Oh yeah, we had us a donnybrook."

"She hates it when I speak of Uncle Stan."

"Yes, she does."

"Beth and I represent the present and future generation of Buckleys. I'm interested in my forebears at every level. Beth's family history is cut and dried, as is Mom's. It's the Buckley side that is murky."

"Murky's putting it mildly," Buckley said. "Murky as the black lagoon on a moonless night."

"Frankly, genealogical curiosity isn't my exclusive motive. The lifespan of family tree members can provide a vital clue to one's own longevity probabilities. You can live the healthiest life possible, but if you're predisposed to a condition, your preventive measures will likely be fruitless."

Buckley knew where this was going. "My mother was no angel. I haven't the foggiest notion who my dad was. I'm the only Buckley I know of who reached my present age."

"No idea whatsoever regarding your father?"

"Nope. And for the record, I'm not blaming him, whoever he is, for *my* lousy track record as a father. Like yourself, I did better growing up without one."

"Did Uncle Stan and you have the same father?"

"We were never certain. Mom would say yes, Mom would say no. It was rare that she was in any condition to give a straight answer on any topic."

"Hmm," Stanley replied.

End of subject, Buckley hoped.

"Say, how long you had the Corvette?"

"A year. I've always liked cars."

"A fact I should've known but didn't take the trouble to," Buckley thought out loud, immediately regretting that he had.

Stan lifted both hands from the wheel, a gesture of cool Buckley didn't think he had in him, and added, "I've told my namesake story to my friends and acquaintances in IT. They tend to be insular. It comes from the single-mindedness and the seventy-hour weeks."

"Eye-what?"

"Information technology. Computers. Software. I love their reaction. They have an increased respect for, or rather, a wariness of my gene pool. Doesn't hurt at all when you sit down to negotiate."

"In business you need every edge you can get," Buckley advised.

"What type of restaurant do you own?"

"A small operation. We specialize in regional cooking and are tourist friendly."

"Sounds like a winner. I researched newspaper clippings. I found a picture of Uncle Stan on the sidewalk covered by a sheet. Mom freaked out."

"Your Uncle Stan was a violent death waiting to happen, except he didn't know it. If he hadn't of gotten in a jackpot then, he would sooner or later."

They emerged from the funnel. The Seattle skyline blocked the early dusk. Lights burned in thousands and thousands of offices. Buckley resisted the urge to gawk. Since stepping on U.S. soil, he was aware that he acted at times like a visitor from either West Hayseed or Mars.

"When is your flight?"

"I'd have to check my ticket. No hurry."

"I researched Belize online," Stan said.

"As a vacation or a more permanent situation, Belize's damn hard to beat."

"Belize. A parliamentary democracy," Stan recited. "Chief crops: Sugar, citrus, bananas. Chief industries: Garments, tourism, and foodstuffs. Per capita GDP, a hair under three thousand dollars. One hundred and fourteen television sets per one thousand people."

"Very good," Buckley said. "Excellent."

"One TV for every ten people isn't many. I didn't see a stat for computers, but they have good websites. Belize seems to be wired."

"Yep, we definitely are," said the computerphobic Buckley. "We're right up to date computerwise."

"You said Belize is hard to beat. Why?"

"Well, let's see. You wake up every morning to a day not too different than the day before. If somebody's angry with you and you settle the dispute, it stays settled. Haven't had snow since the last Ice Age. Orchids grow wild. Orange trees produce two crops a year. A cold Belikin brew on a verandah on a warm afternoon is lovely. And the birds."

"The birds?"

"Yeah. Color by Technicolor. The nearer to the Equator, the more color in the flora and fauna. That's a known fact. Go out with your binoculars and in fifteen minutes you'll see birds every color in the rainbow."

If the boy was impressed, he didn't show it.

"How do you fly from Seattle to there?"

"Through Houston. Dallas will work too. I'm making an intermediate stopover in Portland to handle some business."

"Sea-Tac to Portland is a shuttle. A half-hour flight running every half-hour. Have you eaten?"

Buckley patted his stomach. "Come to think of it, I

haven't."

"I know this pool hall downtown. Before sjbWare expanded and moved to the Eastside, we had a dumpy second floor office on the next block. They make super pizza."

"Talked me into it," Buckley said. "Pizza's my favorite vegetable."

# 9.

It wasn't downtown, not per se, but just north of it, Stan told him, in a gentrifying neighborhood in transition called Belltown. In transition was right, Buckley noted. A union hall beside a boutique. A homeless guy sacked out in a doorway, a Lexus parked in front. Another guy taking a leak by an auto repair shop, which was up the block from a restaurant with a cutesy name in neon and candles on white tablecloths.

Despite the pool hall being a yuppie hangout for boys and girls Stan's age and younger, the atmosphere was on the money. Faint lighting, fake Tiffany lamps above nine-foot tables, a clinging aroma of stale beer.

Buckley flashed back to any number of scuzzy boomtown bars that attached themselves to Army posts like leeches. The difference here was, nobody smoked and nobody wore a uniform, unless you counted pen protectors and thick glasses. Buckley gauged the clientele as 50-percent propellerhead.

The clientele percentage that turned and stared when they entered was closer to 90. This gave the paranoid Buckley the willies until he realized they were looking at his son, not him. They were looking at him like you'd look at a ballplayer or an actor who'd just moseyed in. Stan was semi-famous and he didn't seem to know or care.

They found a table and ordered a large pepperoni and mushroom, and a pitcher of microbrew so dark you couldn't see light through it. The suds were okay, but Buckley was mildly homesick for an ice-cold Belikin on a hellishly hot day. He wasn't complaining, though. Father and son doing what they termed male bonding, Buckley was on top of the world.

"So what is it your company sells to boost computers?" he asked. "Only boosting I ever did was hubcaps."

Stan Buckley smiled. "Our bread and butter technology is MDAC."

"Em-dac?"

"Most Direct Access Compression. Are you familiar with the technology?"

"Can't quite put my finger on it," Buckley said.

"Well, I'll draw an analogy, a map of Los Angeles."

"La La Land," Buckley said. "Where Andrew bugged out to."

"Yes. Picture the internal workings of a computer as a contiguous Los Angeles map that blankets the surface of the Earth, looping and repeating itself, with the concomitant congestion, dead ends, cul-de-sacs, crisscrossing freeways, and natural obstacles such as hills.

"MDAC technology extends the dead ends into connecting streets, tunnels the hills, reroutes the freeways on a complementary grid, and distributes the traffic evenly. MDAC simultaneously compresses the Earth to the size of Mars. As the reduction factor is three-point-five, the analogy is appropriate."

"No speed bumps," Buckley said. "Shortcuts galore. You never hit a red light."

"Precisely."

"It must've taken tremendous brainpower and your nose to the grindstone to come up with your booster. How'd you start?"

"In the short version, I spent my adolescence at my computer screen. I had no life, as they say, nor did I desire one. You've heard of those rags to riches garage start-ups. I literally started in our garage. Computer slowness frustrated me to the point of obsession. This was while

Mom was married to Jesse."

"The body and fender fella?"

"No. Jesse was a cable TV installer. He was an okay guy and good at electronics. What was to become Boost came much later. The technology was incredibly complex and headway was slow. I taught myself programming and made a little money consulting, enough to put myself through a year at the University of Washington. Mom wasn't happy when I left."

Buckley shrugged. "Bill Gates and the rest of those guys, they dropped out of college too, didn't they?"

"Actually, I flunked out. I was too preoccupied by my personal projects to attend class. Mom freaked. In high school, she would threaten to paddle my butt if I brought home lower than a B.

"sjbWare was born in that garage. Jesse was gone by then. I acquired a few employees. We brought out modest versions of sjbBoost and moved to an affordable commercial building, over by where Boeing headquarters used to be. Boost's capabilities were limited. We developed other software. These were specialized applications that paid the bills and not always promptly.

"We threw the dice and leased the space up the street. It was umpteen bucks, but we needed the room. Boost 2.0 was in beta stage. We timed an IPO for 2.0's release."

The last two sentences flew 10,000 feet over Buckley's head. He nodded eagerly and said, "Good move?"

"It turned out to be," Stan said, drinking and continuing with a foam mustache. "We released it late, but as 2.1. The original was buggy and didn't have the features that shot 2.1 to the head of the pack."

"Yeah," Buckley said. "Okay. Way to go."

"This was at the genesis of the dot-com frenzy. "sjbWare stock split six times prior to the NASDAQ meltdown. We moved across the pond to our current location."

Buckley said. "Man, I can't begin to tell you how proud I am."

"I didn't do it alone. Mom was extremely supportive early on. She had financial and personal problems that didn't impede assistance whenever she sensed I needed it. Our first server blew and she maxxed out her plastic to finance a replacement."

"Your mom's a helluva lady," Buckley said, clinking Stan's glass in toast.

"I didn't accomplish product development alone either. The 2.1 thrust came from a team of software designers. I'd been on the right track, but lacked the sheer number crunching and programming requirements myself. It was less a breakthrough than an evolutionary collaboration, an empirical and research-driven push to the top of the hill."

"I find that's usually the best approach too," Buckley said.

"Beth came aboard around that time. She was instrumental in eliminating bugs and other bumps in the road."

"Your wife Beth?"

Stan raised his glass like an ICBM lifting off.

"Her bandwidth's outta sight."

"Bandwidth," Buckley said, nodding. "You can't go far in this day and age without bandwidth."

His son had been eyeing the billiards tables and asked, "Do you shoot pool?"

"I used to shoot a pretty decent stick in the Army. It's been years."

"How decent is decent?"

"We'd play for a beer and a quarter and sometimes a buck, which was a heavy bet on GI's pay in the 1960s. If I was on, I could play and drink on someone else's money and have a nice meal afterwards."

"I have a professional table in the basement. The slate's an inch thick. I've used it twice. I have no time."

A basement too. The roots of the toadstools.

Buckley said, standing up. "C'mon. You have time now."

They played eight ball. Stan beat him legitimately in the first game, a frustrating marathon where it seemed the balls would never fall in for father or son.

In the second, Buckley partially regained his stroke. Most every shot dropped except the long diagonals. Stan improved too, although his game was reactive. He'd make the ball, but couldn't or wouldn't position the cue ball for the next shot. You'd think a software brainiac would plan four shots ahead; the best players treated pool as a chess match.

In game three, Buckley was in a groove, well on his way to running the table, then got greedy on a combination and knocked in the eight ball.

"Did you lose on purpose?" Stan asked as Buckley racked the balls.

"Go in the tank? Not a chance. If you were two years old, I'd throw the game. Maybe."

Buckley had noticed four young guys in a booth observing them shoot while draining pitchers at a rapid clip, like a frat house drinking contest. They were obviously grouchy, giving his boy the stink-eye, and now two of them were standing over Buckley as he carefully lifted the triangle from the balls. One said, "Challenge the table?"

He was the smaller of the pair, a thin-faced sport who had a shaved head, rimless glasses and a goatee meant to make him look fierce. All it did in Buckley's opinion was draw attention to a weak chin. His partner was towering and pear-shaped, an earring accenting a long, greasy ponytail. They carried cue sticks and wore T-shirts of some raggedy rock band.

"No thanks, Partlow," Stan answered quickly.

"Ten bucks a game. Make it interesting."

"This is a private game."

"Ten measly bucks. You can afford a little wager, can't you, Buckley?"

Buckley had thought for an instant this clown Partlow was challenging him, but it was his boy he was glaring daggers at. Stan ignored him as he leaned over to make the break. Buckley had to bite his tongue and not tell Partlow to clean the wax out of his ears, he had his answer.

The stick skittered off the cue ball — not enough chalk — so the balls separated halfheartedly. The five somehow fell. Stan badly missed an easy shot on the nine in a corner pocket and told his father, "You have the stripes."

"He's a billionaire," Partlow told his partner, louder than necessary. "And ten bucks a game is too rich for his blood."

Billionaire. Jesus H. Christ. Could this *really* be true? Buckley couldn't visualize how many zeros there were in a billion.

"Lucky for us Buckley chickened out, dude. He'd figure how to fuck us over again."

"Yeah. Again. The chickenshit."

"Cluck cluck cluck," said Partlow, flapping bent arms.

Buckley had had enough.

"Who are these assholes?" he asked Stan, also at higher than conversational volume.

"They used to work for me. You have the stripes."

Okay, fine, a subject Stan didn't wish to pursue. Buckley circled the table to analyze the layout and to test if their visitors would move out of his path. They did, by a whisker.

"Who're you calling an asshole?" said Partlow's large friend.

Buckley ignored him and laid his cue on the table. They could wait until he was good and ready to resume shooting.

He sat with his son and drank his beer.

"I know curiosity killed the cat, but what's the deal on the Bobbsey Twins?"

"Shortly before the IPO and the move, I fired them. Partlow and the big one, Boswell."

"He's long past due for a shampoo and haircut. Their pals at the table?"

"One I don't know. The other, Cline, I canned too."

"Was that this downsizing you see all over the news?"

"No. Fired. We were expanding, not laying off people. They spent more time in here than working. They may have had industrial espionage on their plates too. I can't prove it. I'm sorry we ran into them. I thought they'd gotten on with their lives."

"Don't apologize. It's a free country and I have the stripes," Buckley said, getting up and chalking his cue. "That mess you left me on the break, thanks a bunch."

Stan laughed, a genuine laugh. Buckley didn't have a promising shot, so he drilled the cue ball into the logjam. They caromed every which way. A solid rolled into a side pocket.

"This is your lucky game," Buckley told Stan.

"Better to be lucky than good," Partlow said. "Ask Mister Buckley, sir. He should know."

"Don't recall addressing you," Buckley said.

"I don't recall anybody explaining 'assholes' to my satisfaction," Boswell said, looking at him. "This is a reasonable inquiry."

"Also known an anus and other things. Everybody's got one," Buckley said, studying the table. "You're the exception to the rule. You got a second one. It's underneath your nose. You oughta join the circus and all you duds oughta switch over to coffee or soda pop, something you can handle."

Stan was on his feet. "You guys want to leave him alone? Your problem concerns me."

Buckley smiled at Boswell until he averted his eyes.

"He shouldn't be referring to people as assholes," Boswell told Stan. "Assholes who have morphed into duds."

Partlow got into Stan's face. "We never had our exit interview. Let's have it now."

"You missed the appointment."

Partlow jabbed his finger in Stan's midsection. "How about my exit interview right fucking *now*."

Stan brushed his finger aside. "You were a malingering boozer, Partlow, you and Boswell and Cline. You were useless on the beta rollout, when we desperately needed you. You assumed somebody else would do the work and if it panned out, stock options would land in your laps merely because you were on the payroll."

Buckley did not comprehend a single word of Partlow's noisy, comeback, other than it was work-related. He was ragging Stan on modular codes and streaming data and dual-pane interfaces, on paradigms and multi-tiered architecture, technical shit Buckley didn't know from Shinola.

Buckley admired his kid's spunk, but the two of them, they looked like girls squared off at recess. If he stepped in between them like a playground monitor, Stan would never speak to him again.

The two guys at the table rose to their feet and Boswell began slowly creeping around the table behind Stan, a sneaky mismatch organizing.

Four against one. This changed the rules of engagement.

Buckley headed Boswell off. "Far enough."

"Mind your own business, Pops."

While the mopes at the table hadn't advanced, they remained on their feet.

Buckley told Boswell, "Kiss off, Rapunzel."

Boswell pursed his lips and slowly shook his head, stunned by the ongoing disrespect from the geezer.

Stan was bent over the table, lining up the seven-ball, basically dismissing his tormentor. Stan was silently saying that he'd had a bellyful, that Partlow wasn't worth the time of day, that he was lower than snakeshit.

In the old days, Buckley thought, we had us a prelude to sirens and helmeted MPs. Now, it'd be sirens and Seattle's finest.

Swell.

The Buckley desperado gene at work.

"How's that cunt you promoted into holy matrimony?" Partlow said. "Is the nooky worth it?"

Stan sprang upright, clenched his eyes, and threw a flailing combination of sidearm blows that caught Partlow by surprise, slamming him against the table, his head gonging the Tiffany.

Before Buckley could yell "Atta boy!", Boswell elbowed his ribs and steamed ahead to aid his pal. Buckley gasped, grabbed long, trailing hair, and allowed his legs to go limp. They hit the floor together and hard, Boswell screaming and conking his head on the side of the pool table.

Buckley scrambled out from under the yowling, writhing tub of lard and retrieved his cue. The activity had frozen Cline and friend. They were chunky bookends, much of it blubber. When they saw Buckley in a crouch, they advanced.

Using the stick as a cane, Buckley raised himself upright and assumed a batter's stance, butt end out. "Which one of you dick lickers wants to step up to the plate and be a ground rule double?"

He took a cut, a serious whiff that raised a breeze inches from Cline's face.

"Think I'm bullshitting?"

They backpedaled and stumbled into their seats.

Buckley saluted them. "Drink your beer and mind your own fucking business. Just trying to keep it a fair fight."

Stan and Partlow were exhausted, in a nose-to-nose clinch, as if hockey players, doing little further damage. They were a mess, dripping blood, drool and snot.

Stan Buckley, by God, had the definite advantage!

Meanwhile, Boswell was moving groggily on his knees, clutching at Stan's ankles. Buckley returned the rib-cage favor with a swift kick that slumped him like a pile of dirty laundry.

They had a rapt and shocked audience, customers and employees alike. A guy yelled to Stan that he'd be his witness if anything happened, followed by a loose chorus of "yeahs." An especially tense barmaid held her drink tray paddle-fashion, tempted to plow in and break it up.

"Will someone please call nine-one-one," she finally cried.

Buckley easily separated the pathetic pugilists. They could barely hold their arms up. Firm hand on his shoulder, Buckley parted the crowd and led his son outside, saying, "They have nine-one-one in Belize too, only you dial nine-zero. How fast do they respond in Seattle?"

"Thooper thast," Stanley said.

"I hear sirens."

"Therth always thyrens in downtown Theattle."

Buckley picked up the pace. "No sense tempting fate."

"Got to thook."

"Huh?"

"Thook."

"What's thook?"

"Thook. I'm going to be thick."

"Puke?" Buckley said. "Puke?"

"Uh," Stan said, gulping.

"Thisaway," Buckley said, steering him into an alley, where he leaned on a Dumpster and indeed barfed his guts out. He was unsteady and Buckley hovered, available if the boy lost his balance. Not much of a fathering substitute for bedtime stories and driving instruction, he knew. It'd have to do.

When he was done, Buckley asked, "You okay?"

Stan dabbed running nose and eyes with a handkerchief. "I'll thurvive."

Old-fashioned male bonding is what this was, before you heard the word "bond" associated with other than Wall Street and fine bourbon. Here they were, in a dimly lit alley, in the shadow of a Dumpster, two warriors who had defended a lady's honor. This was the stuff of legend.

Unfortunately, it was also the stuff of divorces.

He said, "You did damn good in there. Damn good."

Stan ran his tongue over his lips. "Thankth. How'th my mouth look?"

Buckley squinted. A lower corner was swollen. A classic fat lip. Bad news.

"The light's lousy," he evaded. "You're sounding clearer and some liquid will cure the rasp."

"Beth will kill me."

"Hey, if you decide to go the truthful route, that was her honor you defended. Somebody got in my face and called your mom a cunt, one of us would be going to the hospital."

"Decepthun ithn't a good way to thart a marriage."

Buckley let that one alone.

"After those jerks let uth down, I don't think I could've made the 2.1 deadline without her. Beth wath tremendouth."

"Can't beat bandwidth mixed with hormones." Buckley cocked a thumb at the sooty brick wall, the direction of the pool hall. "I rest my case. It wasn't your fault. Those rinky-dink duds started the fracas."

"I've been in thimilar confrontations perhapth twyth in my life. I walked away. I don't know what got into me. Nevertheleth, Beth will blame you, whith is grothly unthair. Mom too. I brought you. You thould be on your plane. I thould be home. How're you doing, inthidentally?"

The boy already had the earmarks of being pussywhipped, in retrospect not an entirely terrible thing. "Other than feeling old and sore and decrepit, in the pink. You're sounding kind of normal. I understood almost every word. Seriously, blame me. No problem. I'll be gone soon."

"It wouldn't be right."

"Susan taught you right and wrong," Buckley said. "She had less luck in that area with me."

"We'll thee."

"I'd consider it an honor to take the rap."

"Anyhow, I appretheate you covering my backthide. Boswell's a nasty pieth of work."

Buckley almost said that's what dads are for. Not the proper moment. If ever.

"I did what anybody'd do," Buckley said modestly as he massaged his ribs. "Except for going against my policy and giving Ponytail the first whack. I should've seen it coming. I'm not as young as I used to be. I can't afford to give up the advantage. Not that I engage in fisticuffs on a regular basis."

Rustling noises came from inside or under the Dumpster. Father and son started for the sidewalk.

"You did thooper," Stan said. "Boswell's twith your size and half your age."

"Does that mean I got bandwidth?"

Stan winced as he laughed.

"The advantage of reaching a certain age is that you lose crazy notions, like having to fight fair. I got an idea how you can make up with Beth. Flowers."

"It's worth a try. Did flowerth do the trick for you with Mom?"

"Nah. By then my bridges were burned. They were ashes. Burned right down to the waterline."

# 10.

Stan knew a florist shop between downtown Seattle and the airport that stayed open late. He paid a mint for a bouquet that required both hands to carry and filled the Vette's microscopic trunk. Every color that existed in nature and some that didn't, Buckley thought as he inhaled a perfume store's worth of fragrance. He couldn't identify the flowers, but had seen some in Belize, growing wild. If this portable botanical garden didn't ring Beth's chimes, Buckley might never be a grandpa.

At a 24-hour restaurant that served breakfast anytime, they ordered plates of eggs and pancakes and hash browns and bacon. They hadn't finished their first slice of pizza at the billiard parlor before the rude interruption. Stan was especially famished for obvious reasons, having burned calories he didn't customarily burn.

They were so near Seattle-Tacoma International Airport that departing jets made the window at their booth hum. Buckley suggested moving to the bar where they could hear themselves think. He waved off the waitress's coffeepot and further suggested Bloody Marys in the cocktail lounge. "I have rigor mortis setting in and you look a little peaked."

"It isn't too early or too late for hair of the dog," Father further advised Son from a barstool. "The Bloody Mary is therapeutic, vitamin-packed, and your wife won't smell the vodka on you."

"Maybe just one," Stan said. "When our food comes."

His lisping and hoarseness were almost gone, but the fat lip would require more time, much more. He'd been to the bathroom to clean up and knew with his own eyes, which explained his long face.

Buckley said, "Waiting is probably smart. The dry heaves are no fun."

Stan touched his lip glumly.

"Ice will bring down the swelling," Buckley said.

"Not sufficiently."

Buckley winked. "Your half of the Bobbsey Twins, Paperclip or whatever his name is, I bet he looks fifty times worse. His own mother won't recognize him, poor bastard."

Stan forced a smile and lifted his glass.

"Play your cards right and they'll want to mother you when something like this takes place where you're a totally innocent victim who got bunged up," Buckley recommended. "If Beth isn't adverse to strong language, tell her what that mope called her."

Stan pondered for a moment. "People said Partlow was sweet on her when he was with the company."

"There you go," Buckley said. "How innocent can you be?"

Stan didn't reply.

"You got justice and honor going for you and a trunkful of flowers."

"We'll see," Stan said unenthusiastically.

"Of course, if these types of situations become repetitious, they're bound to be cranky irregardless if you're married to them or not. I know this to be a fact."

Having said plenty and then some, Buckley stirred his drink with the accompanying pickled green bean, took a sip and a bite, glanced at a TV suspended above the backbar, and saw a young PFC Joseph Buckley in Army uniform. Buckley blinked and PFC Buckley zoomed into the background, a screen within a screen, flanked by two commentators in tall wooden chairs, one male and one female.

Buckley spit out the string bean. "Holy fucking cow!"

He had watched *Exclusive!!*, this tabloid news show, in Belize. They piped it in via satellite. Their typical fare was trailer park incest, spanking judges, and cattle mutilations. The girl cutie was a perky blonde who wore mini-skirts and recrossed her legs at least once per segment. Buckley held to the theory that their ratings were so high because of peekaboo expectations. Otherwise, the programs were so god-awful dumb, they bypassed entertainment, sailing a mile over the top.

Stan gaped, then asked, "You?"

It had been snapped at Fort Ord. A photographer had come through and taken pictures of the unit and the individual troops, hopeful for orders. This was Susan's favorite military shot of Buckley. She thought his lopsided smile was sexy. "I was a pencilneck those days, but I'd recognize that schnoz anywhere."

"The picture," Stan said. "I've seen that photo."

Buckley held a finger to his lips.

*Exclusive!!*'s hosts were chattering, muted. The remote control was beside a container of maraschino cherries. Buckley snatched it and studied the confusion of buttons. "Volume?"

"Here." Stan drummed on the remote with a thumb. Horizontal red bars expanded across the bottom of the screen.

"– U.S. Army sharpshooter and Vietnam combat veteran who disappeared and is believed to have defected to Cuba in the mid-1960's," said the male cutie, who had a coiffure out of a Jell-O mold and blinding teeth.

Frowning in concern, his colleague added, "Brett, I'm disturbed that if these allegations are true, Private First Class Joseph J. Buckley served our country undetected."

"Ironically, thirty-three months following that fateful day, Kelli."

"That photograph is so familiar," Stan said.

"Sharpshooter," Buckley muttered. "I couldn't hit the broad side of a barn. I couldn't hit a bull in the butt with a bazooka."

"What's this about?" Stan whispered.

The Zapruder film rolled in fuzzy, blotchy color. The motorcade, the Lincoln limo, JFK's head jerking. Jackie Kennedy in pink, confused, reacting.

"I don't think I want to know," Buckley said.

Young PFC Buckley and the cuties returned, a grinning threesome.

Stan snapped his fingers. "Mom has that same picture."

"There are too many coincidences in this scenario to suit me," Kelli told Brett.

"Amen," Buckley told the television set.

The jukebox came on, a twangy country lament that sounded to Buckley as if a blowtorch was being held to the singer's privates. He craned his neck to hear.

"*Exclusive!!* Has learned exclusively that Buckley may have reentered the country clandestinely from Cuba —"

Stan said, "Cuba?"

"Guano," Buckley yelled. "Bat guano."

"Shhhh," Stan said, wincing.

"On that fateful November day in 1963."

"They're bouncing around chronologically," Stan said, frowning. "What are we missing?"

"— circumstantial and thin, yes. However, the violent incident documented the prior night at the infamous Carousel Club."

"Undeniably, Brett. Although neither Jack Ruby nor PFC Buckley nor his soldier companion filed charges, ironically, the incident was reported to the Dallas Police Department, as you'll see by this exclusive copy of the incident report."

Buckley squinted at the unreadable printed form Kelly dangled and did not even notice her recrossing her legs.

"A conspiracy in the most infamous act of political assassination in our nation's history?"

"Political, hell," Buckley mumbled. "Me political? I've never even voted."

Stan asked, "They're accusing you of conspiracy in the JFK assassination?"

"— too soon to place at the grassy knoll and to make accusations."

"Wouldn't know the grassy knoll if it jumped up and bit me," Buckley said, shaking his head.

They flashed mug shots of brother Stan, front and profile. Big Stan was fuller in the face than Buckley was now. Had he survived his own craziness he'd be porky. That trademark thrust of the jaw was apparent. Buckley always wondered whether it was bone structure or part of his brother's tough-guy routine.

He downed his drink and signaled for a refill.

"I have those mug shots of Uncle Stan copied from microfiche," Stan said.

"— a family legacy of criminality and violence."

"The person who supplied the photograph of former Private First Class Buckley and the vital documents understandably wishes to remain anonymous."

" — tomorrow's special edition will feature an exclusive interview that hopefully fits the pieces of this puzzle, a startling revelation including the identification of an emblem signifying membership in a secret organization and clues to Joseph J. Buckley's whereabouts."

Their food arrived as the show went to final commercials.

Buckley dug into his eggs.

Stan looked at him and said, "How can you eat?"

"Because I'm hungry."

"Shouldn't we be making ourselves scarce?"

"What for? They've gotten as far as late '65, early '66. I've changed some. I have a head start."

"You can tell me about it or not. I can't see you as party to, you know. "

"High treason? Gimme a break. I was a cook, for Chrissake. I may've poisoned a few folks, but not on purpose, and I was no Commie. I was in Dallas that weekend. They have me on that count. I'm trying to put two and two together. The photo of me your mother had, are you sure it's the same one?"

"Absolutely."

"Me too."

"She had it in a frame on her dresser."

"No kidding?"

"Well, between husbands."

"When's the last time you saw it?"

They looked at each other and said in unison, "Andrew."

"Who else?" Buckley said. "Your mother's diaries. Their mystery man's documents. Bingo."

Stan said. "I can remember her in the evening, writing and writing and writing. By now, she's compiled the world's longest autobiography. I wasn't aware you knew each other in 1963?"

"We didn't. We met not long after I, uh, became a civilian. We discussed our pasts, as people do."

"If we're correct about Andrew, how is he pulling this off?"

Buckley shrugged. "On the basis of diaries and a picture, the rascal definitely sold them a load of manure."

"Did I hear the host refer to an emblem signifying a secret organization?"

"Yeah, and I have a fairly good idea what that is."

Stan waited.

Buckley shoveled hash browns into his mouth and said, "The good news is that they haven't connected you to me. Finish your food. You need your nourishment."

Stan Buckley listlessly obeyed his biological father.

Outside, after they ate, Buckley rolled up his sleeve and revealed the headless American eagle. "It's faded and wrinkly, but this here is the secret club emblem Andrew and those talking haircuts dreamed up."

Stan started the Corvette. "The obvious question."

"Why no head on the eagle? Your Mom asked that the first time she saw it too."

Buckley savored the memory, since it was also the first time Susan had seen the rest of him unclothed. "A legit question requiring a lengthy reply."

Stan carefully licked his smashed lip. "We have the time."

"I was stationed at Fort Bliss, Texas, outside of El Paso," Buckley began. "My buddy and I who I worked together with at the consolidated mess hall, we were able to wangle three-day passes and decided we wanted to go on up to Dallas, basically for the hell of it on account of neither of us had been there. This buddy was Dave Kenworthy, who I mentioned had the red-and-white Corvette and the bad luck in Vietnam.

"Well, Texas is a big state and not all the freeways were in yet. GI's have to eat three squares every day, so cooks rotate long shifts, sort of like firemen do. Our extended weekend happened to be Wednesday night through Sunday morning. We took turns driving straight through, about thirteen hours, if I recall.

"I won't beat around the bush. We were young troops with only a couple of things on our minds while on pass. Our barhopping came to concentrate on strip joints. This dump in particular, I don't recollect how the trouble developed, but one thing led to another involving Dave and the club owner, who enjoyed being his own bouncer.

"Maybe Dave was too grabby with one of his girls. I don't know. I stepped in between to make peace and caught a rabbit punch from the owner, kind of like what I allowed myself to take tonight. Then I got in a lick or two on him.

"He was a insane, yappy little character, stocky and strong as an ox. The bunch of us went tumbling down the stairs, out onto the sidewalk like a gunnysack full of tomcats. The cops came and filed a report. They knew the owner on a friendly basis and were used to this sort of thing. Jack Ruby had cooled off by then. We were lucky we weren't hauled in."

Stan said, "Your presence in the Carousel Club was random."

"It was. Are you up to speed on the events?"

Stan pulled onto the highway. "The highlights. Before I flunked out, I took a class in American history and I had a college friend who was a conspiracy buff."

Buckley said, "It really was strictly random, us at the Carousel. I didn't know Jack Ruby from Jack Squat till he plugged Oswald a few days later. He was an aggressive, feisty son of a bitch, a dirty fighter and mean as a rattler. Can't even imagine what was going through the man's noggin."

"What is the significance of your headless eagle?"

"Tattoos are something you only used to get done when you were in the service. These kids here I've seen since being back in the States, girls *and* boys, earrings all over their faces too. Don't get me going on that topic.

"Anyway, tattooing involves a certain threshold of drunkenness. We attained that level the next day also. When you're on a three-day pass, it's always cocktail hour. That's just how it is.

"We were at this hole-in-the-wall tattoo parlor, which

as it turns out, was not a great distance from Dealey Plaza. Dave picked out a snake wrapped around a sword or some such and I went for the eagle. I was a lifer then, gung ho in my own manner, as gung ho as a cook and malingerer can possibly be. It was my turn. In a while, sirens began howling from every direction. People were outside talking. This was lunchtime or slightly later. The artist had gotten as far as what you see on my arm today and went out to investigate.

"He came back in and said the President of the United States had been shot. He was in Dallas, I asked? I wasn't much a newspaper reader in those days, beyond the sports and funnies. The artist was kind of in shock even though he said he had his heart set on Goldwater in '64. He shut down and said to come back later."

"You didn't."

"I had the best of intentions. Then we met these two ladies, another story altogether. Next day, driving out of town for Bliss, we went looking for the tattoo place. I guess we kind of forgot where it was. At least I hadn't paid him yet. I figured I had me a conversation piece. Damned if it isn't. A helluva lot more conversation than I bargained for, huh?"

Stan said, "Those tabloid shows are submoronic and amoral, but I can't conceive Andrew milking this any further. It's so thin."

"Revenge must be sweet."

"You were in the wrong place at the wrong time."

"The story of my life," Buckley said.

"I'm afraid your desertion gave that preposterous story currency."

"Yeah. They called it defection. Cuba. They gotta be joking."

"What'll you do?"

"Damned if I know. Hey, isn't the airport back that way, where the planes are taking off?"

"We're not going to the airport. We're going home."

# 11.

"**N**ow, if you decide that telling the truth, the whole truth, and nothing but the truth might blow up in your face, it's not impossible to tiptoe in late, undetected. It can be done," Buckley said, dispensing fatherly advice. "Silence is the key."

"It's not that late, is it?" Stan said. "Beth will be waiting up. I don't know what to do."

"Quarter past after eleven," Buckley said, checking his watch. "Time flies."

Stan groaned. "That is late and she will be waiting up. She's probably worried sick."

They were across the bridge, not far from the Buckley estate. Traffic had thinned, but drivers were still out in force by Belizean standards. Down there, you earned a fraction as much on your job and gas cost double what it did the States, so not too many folks tooled around aimlessly, day and night.

"I believe in thinking positive in these situations. The consequences are hardly ever as bad as you think they'll be."

"I didn't bring a cell phone," Stan said. "That's not like me, but it's no excuse for not calling. Wait, there may be one in the glove box."

Buckley checked. Sure enough. The contraption was twice the size of a candy bar.

He said, "These things are getting to be everywhere, breeding like mice and shrinking at the same time."

"May I have it, please?"

The boy was a moneybags and had an IQ of 300, and

he knows even less about women than I do, Buckley thought. Must come from living your life at a computer screen.

He said, "You're calling her this late to say you're gonna be late? My experience is that you have to explain twice, now and later in person, when they're even grumpier."

Stan digested his father's logic and didn't ask for the baby telephone. Buckley closed the glove box on it and said, "Okay, let's say Beth dozed off on the couch waiting for you. You have a big house. Flank her and hop into bed. She'll come in and say where were you? You can say where the hell were you? I've been here. If she's in bed at the time, you can say, oh, I was in the bathroom. This depends on her being asleep and as a newlywed, well, frankly the odds aren't the greatest."

Stan brushed his fat lip with his pinkie. "How do I deal with this issue?"

"In the morning the swelling oughta be down more. She might not faint dead away. You'll have time to think up a story. You know, like a black eye caused by walking into a door."

"A modest consolation."

Buckley resisted telling him not to pick at his lip. "We definitely had us an unusual evening, extenuating circumstances coming out of our ears. She'll be reasonable, she'll cut you some slack."

Stan turned onto his property and jabbed a gadget clipped to the dashboard. The gate purred open.

"I guess you have alarms too," Buckley said.

"State of the art."

"Camera?"

"Beth is arranging to have surveillance cameras installed."

"Lucky timing for us. While they're here, you might

have them check out the people gate. You don't want folks like me just walking on in."

Stan Buckley looked at him.

Joe Buckley shrugged.

Inside, Buckley said, "If it was me, I'd probably be shutting down the engine and lights, and coasting."

"Isn't that carrying deviousness to the extreme?"

"I'd call it self-preservation."

Stan Buckley shut off the engine and lights, and coasted in neutral down the driveway, tapping the brake. "She'll be doubly angry if we're caught."

"You're being considerate, trying not to wake anyone."

Stan shook his head. "You have an answer for everything."

Stung harder than Ponytail's shot to his ribs, Buckley didn't reply. He had it coming. In the fatherly wisdom department, this kind of clandestine bullshit was all he had to pass along.

The boy did quietly shut his car door, get on his tiptoes, use a key, and roll up the garage manually. They pushed the Corvette in and were spared an awkward goodnight by the harsh blinking of fluorescent lights.

Susan stood next to the switch, wearing a bathrobe and a worried scowl.

"Waiting up, Sooz?" Like my mother never did, Buckley thought.

"I heard the gate open and saw you coasting in the dark. I saw the passenger and knew who it was. I just knew. That stunt has a juvenile signature I'll never forget. Why aren't you airborne somewhere?"

"Cuz I'm here, your basic bad penny."

"Buckley, do you realize what kind of trouble you're in?"

"What else is new?"

"I'm referring a breaking development in the odyssey

of ex-PFC Joseph J. Buckley."

Odyssey. Sooz and her fancy words.

"You been watching trash television. You should be tuned to the public broadcast channel for culture and such."

"First things first. Stanley, why are you cocking your head? Is your neck stiff from driving with the top down? You were always subject to chills."

In slow motion, Stanley Buckley swiveled full face.

Susan's hand went over her opened mouth.

"Oh, good Lord, what happened to you?"

"A long story, Mom."

"I don't doubt it. Wait until Beth she sees you."

"I can wait."

Buckley said, "It wasn't his fault, it wasn't my fault."

"It's never your fault, Joe. It's always the other guy."

"Mom."

"Stanley, don't tell me you walked into a door. That's for black eyes."

"Mom."

"What did he get you mixed up in?"

"Sooz, we were minding our own business having a bite to eat when these jerks picked a fight."

"Out of the clear blue sky, you were challenged to a fistfight?"

"He did what any red-blooded fella would do," Buckley said. "This clown called his brand-new bride a cunt."

"You and your red blood, don't you use that language in front of him!"

"Mom."

"When the hell are you ever going to grow up, Joe Buckley?"

"Mom, it was Partlow and Boswell. He neutralized Boswell, who was going to jump me from behind. Cline and another guy were prepared to pile on too. You remember them."

"I do. They were around sjbWare from the early days, worthless as they come," Susan conceded, throwing Buckley a glance. "Regardless, you have a gift for raising sparks."

"Moving right along," Buckley said. "You saw the TV show too, huh?"

"May I close the garage, please?" Stan asked, doing so.

"Yeah. It's chilly," Buckley said. "Thanks."

Susan said, "I received an anonymous phone call telling me not to miss tonight's *Exclusive!!*."

"What did you anonymous caller sound like?"

"Like Andrew holding cheesecloth over his mouth."

"Which confirms our suspicions," Stan said.

"A mysterious stranger revealing startling news on secret organization symbols crapola," Buckley said, stroking his tattoo.

Susan stepped into fainter light and dabbed her eyes. "I hadn't an inkling Andrew was such a loathsome creature. I suppose it's best I know sooner than later."

Stan asked, "What's his agenda, his bottom line?"

"The infliction of pain," Susan said.

"It's working," Buckley said.

"There's a promised special edition of the show tomorrow night," Stan said.

"Pain and money," Susan said. "I read that those shows pay for quote-unquote information."

"Who's making the popcorn?" Buckley said.

"Andrew's punishing me through you." She looked at her son. "Did you hear the headless eagle saga?"

He nodded. "Bizarre."

"The honest truth," Buckley said, raising his right hand.

"No startling revelations?" she said.

"You know me in the political activism department, Sooz. I've never even voted."

Susan examined her son and twitched her nose. "You come upstairs before you go next door. We can fix the vomit smell, and the blood spatters. A quick toss in the washer and drier. I smell alcohol. Gargle with mouthwash too," She rocked a palm. "Your inflamed lip, I'm not as confident. We can apply a cool compress."

"Mom."

"Listen to your mother. She's a smart lady."

"Buttering me up is pointless, Buckley, if you catch my drift."

"Gotcha. On Andrew, what set him off like this?"

"You know what."

Their old marital telepathy was kicking in. Although the content was faint static, Susan was thinking one thing and saying another. "No. Actually I don't. There's gotta be more. To do what we saw tonight. He's going to a lot of effort. He's going above and beyond. He's a man on a fanatical mission."

Susan sighed. "All right, the last time I saw him, before his sudden trip south, he insisted we elope immediately. Drive immediately to Idaho where there's no waiting period and tie the knot. I said I wanted to do plan it properly. I invariably regret jumping the gun into marriage."

"Did he address the prenup?" Stan broke in.

"The who?"

"A prenuptial agreement that spells out division of property in event of a divorce. Any marriage between people who bring an uneven amount of assets should have a prenup. Beth and I do."

Tattoos galore on kids and marital prenups, Buckley thought. A whole brave new world.

"Stanley insisted that we have one. Excellent advice. Andrew went ballistic. He said I had no respect for him, that I didn't trust him."

"Do you have a theory what Andrew and his hosts have in store for tomorrow night?" her son asked.

"I have a theory what's going on inside Andrew's pointy head. Stanley, did I ever tell you his date of birth?"

"If you did, I wasn't interested enough to listen."

Buckley bit his cheek. A fine lad he had sired.

"November 22, 1963. I know how Andrew's mind works. My diaries and the coincidence of Joe in Dallas, this was providence for him. It is meant to be. And if he identifies himself tomorrow and is convincing, he can promote and advance his art career."

"Which beats going directly to the cops. There'd be nothing in it for him except revenge," Buckley said.

"I imagine Andrew had little difficulty convincing the powers that be on that silly television show. He fancies himself an expert on the assassination, a scholar."

"He's very bright," Buckley said.

"Bud Pogue," his son said. "I'll consult Bud in the morning."

"In the meantime, let's get upstairs to work on your owie."

Stan turned to his father. "If you like, come on in to the office with me tomorrow. Bud Pogue is our chief of site security. He could supply useful input on your issues."

"Thank you. I definitely will."

"Stanley, don't pick at your lip. "We don't want an infection. I have antibiotic ointment."

"Mom, I'd really better go in and see Beth."

"Not until we take care of that lip and your clothes. Besides, she's not there. Beth and Irene went out to dinner and a movie. Didn't you get lucky?"

Buckley watched his boy exhale.

Susan Buckley curled an index finger. Her son finally closed the garage door and moved as if tugged on a leash.

# 12.

It was a dark and stormy morning, not ragtop weather.

So father and son drove to sjbWare in the massive Mercedes-Benz S-class sedan, not the Corvette. Buckley was snugly belted in the soft, temperature-controlled leather seat, the kid on take-your-kid-to-work day. All he needed was a Bugs Bunny lunchbox.

Two fights in less than a week, pitiful as they were. Buckley could barely remember one and you couldn't term the other a genuine fistfight. They were signs that he needed to be home in laid-back Belize, running his business and minding his own business. Add in Susan's crazy boyfriend who was advertising Buckley as Lee Harvey Oswald's blood brother, and it was high time to skedaddle.

Once they assembled the pieces, he'd not only have the Army's attention, there would be the State Department for passport hanky-panky. They'd probably form a new Warren Commission in his honor too. He felt like one of those English foxes, with dandies in red suits on horseback and their mutts nipping at his heels.

Him with Harold Roy Qwerty in his hip pocket, maybe he could swim the Rio Grande. They wouldn't give an old gringo dogpaddling in the wrong direction a second glance. He was just about paranoid enough to try.

"We haven't spoken much about my paternal grandmother," Stan said.

"There isn't a lot to say. She tried in her own way to be a decent person. She scraped by taking in laundry and whatever, honest work, and maybe, just maybe, some forms of income on the side I don't ever wanna know about. You neither. The older I get, the more I realize that with her problems and the fog she usually was in from the sauce, she did the best she could trying to raise your Uncle Stan and me."

"Mom told me you were in the Army when my grandmother passed away."

"I was, in Ord at AIT. That's advanced individual training, for me it was cook's school after Basic. The word came down to me through channels from the Red Cross to our orderly room. They do it like that because you normally get emergency leave and they want confirmation the tragedy's on the up-and-up, not a tall tale. As I can attest to personally, an awful lot of guys in the service did not particularly care to be there."

"You were able to make the funeral, I hope?"

"I was. I flew in to Portland. My mother's sister, Madge, met me. She lived in southern Oregon someplace. It was the second or third and last time I ever saw her. She died in the eighties. The funeral was in Albany, a town an hour out of Portland. There were friends and shirttail relatives in attendance to see off Amy Buckley, maybe thirty total. Some I knew, some I didn't."

"Uncle Stan?"

"My brother was not amongst them. He was incarcerated. What stuck in my mind was that nobody seemed to know anybody else very well. Everybody was a stranger and this made me sad, knowing that she went through life more or less as a stranger herself."

"I occasionally speculate if your biological father was there, perhaps standing in the background."

"Could be, although I would not bet the farm on it."

"How old was my grandmother when she passed away?"

"Good question. Late forties?"

"I have a copy of her death certificate. I can check."

Buckley looked at him.

"Thanks to Bud Pogue," Stan said. "Bud has a wealth of military police and private detective experience. We have another person in charge of electronic security. Our business is dynamic and proprietary. She monitors for outside hacking and employee misuse of the Internet and confidential technology. Bud Pogue is proudly computerphobic."

"A man after my own heart."

"However, Bud is super at keeping unauthorized individuals out and equipment from, shall we say, growing a pair of legs. Bud can be intimidating. He — frightens people."

"A very useful skill to have in his line of work," Buckley said, nodding.

"Indeed. Mom told me you have a personal documentation problem."

"Yes, yes I do. For the benefit of all concerned, I should be working on that now on my way back to Belize."

"As I said last night, Bud may be able to assist on your various issues and the ramifications. Accordingly, let's not be hasty. We'll explore the possibilities. I wouldn't worry excessively yet."

Yet. Buckley was attempting to read his son, dying to figure how it went last night between him and Beth. Beyond not seeing the monster bouquet flung out a window onto the patio or in the garbage, he hadn't a clue. His son played his cards so damn close to the vest.

Buckley edged into the subject. "Hey, your lip's looking a lip instead of a butcher's mistake."

Stan hinted at a smile. "I told Beth the truth."

Buckley cringed.

"I broke the news to her in the dark and said what Partlow called her and how I reacted, how you protected my rear. She hates Partlow's guts. It went as well as could be expected."

"Well, hey, okay, good, great."

Buckley imagined Beth had seen a totally different side of her new husband, her soft-spoken computer fella a rogue out of the days of chivalry like the steroided pirates on the jackets of Susan's romance paperbacks. He noticed that Stan had been sitting up straighter in the car. His posture was as a rule, if you wanted to nit-pick, a little stooped, less than perfect. Buckley kept his big yap shut and let the boy savor what might have taken place in the sack after he spilled the beans.

In Redmond, a 'burb town not far from Microsoft's world headquarters, they pulled into a business park so similar to Dotti Magnuson's, Buckley visualized the big black cubes rolling off an assembly line, robots gluing glass panes onto erector-set girder work.

At the entrance, the sjbWare logo was chiseled into an upright concrete slab the size of a basketball court. Sprinklers were spritzing in the rain, overwatering rolling lawns. Flower plants in loud colors looked like they'd been poked into the bark five minutes ago. Excess water waterfalled off the curbing into the lot.

"Since I got your letter, I've wondered why the parallelograph?"

"The? Oh, right. After computer science, math was my favorite subject in school, and plane geometry was my favorite math course. There's no other significance than it was pleasing to my eye."

Speaking of pleasing to the eye, circling above was a northern harrier. Number 294 on Buckley's life list.

"Once I'm settled in, I'll give you the grand tour and we'll find Bud."

Buckley was curious how he'd be introduced. Father, dad, son, pops, et cetera, had not entered their vernacular.

"Thanks. Which building is yours?"

"Buildings A, B, D, and the upper two floors of H. We sublease C, E and G," Stan said. "We're negotiating to place our International Division into F. They were growing like a weed, but the dot-com fallout may've put that on hold. Last quarter's International's numbers were flat. My office is in A."

"Uh huh," was all Buckley could manage, gawking as Stan parked in front of A. This was no run-of-the-mill business park, this was *his boy's* business park and the lot looked like a European car dealership.

Stan no sooner stepped out of the car than a cluster of happy young folks squeezed out of the main doors, vying to shield their leader with their umbrellas. They sloshed to him through a downpour and a sprinkler flash flood on the pavement. He met them halfway, not caring what it did to his khakis and white sneakers. Sort of reminded Buckley of the I Shall Return pictures of MacArthur wading ashore in the Philippine surf.

Buckley tagged along, dodging the precip the best he could. His wardrobe was not unlimited. Stan and his troops were exchanging high fives, like basketball players. Some looked hazily familiar from the wedding.

He trailed the mob into the building and caught up after they dispersed. "Wedding congrats?"

"No." Stan was walking springier, a borderline swagger, nodding hello left and right. "Last night's brouhaha. Jungle drums travel fast. Many remember last night's antagonists."

Buckley followed him into an elevator, thinking that similarities to Dotti's offices ended when they came through the door. This was an open barn of an office building, not a collection of ritzy suites. Bare bones ugly, no shaggy carpet, no wood paneling. The layout was a warren of cubicles jam-packed full of manuals and beige computer gadgetry, most occupants Stan's age and younger, blue light glowing on their tender faces.

They rode to the fourth and top floor. Stan had the only walled-in office, in a corner, but there were windows on the inside as well as looking out. Buckley thought executives required privacy for some of the stuff they did; he certainly would.

An ordinary placard on the door: STANLEY BUCKLEY

It was a pinprick rather than a stab in the heart. He hadn't expected STAN BUCKLEY and certainly not S. JOSEPH BUCKLEY or S. J. BUCKLEY or best of all, a fantasy S. JOSEPH (JOE) BUCKLEY. It occurred to him that he hadn't heard anyone except Susan address him by his first name.

A florid, middle-aged guy sat inside, trimming his fingernails, letting the clippings fall where they may. He wore a checked sport jacket that matched nothing known to man or nature. A striped tie cinched like a noose in the frayed collar of a pastel shirt. Sideburned hair as white as snow curved over his head and his no neck, the style of an aging stock car racer's.

"Bud Pogue?" Joe Buckley asked Stanley Buckley.

"How'd you know?"

"Lucky guess. The lone necktie on the premises and he's a dead ringer for a Bud Pogue."

His son asked, "Can you hang loose for a minute?"

Buckley waited outside. The minute was ten of them, no end in sight, so he occupied himself by snooping on the floor.

He peeked in on a young lady who had earrings and zits in ample supply.

"What's cookin'?"

Without looking up from line after line of digits and letters, she said, "I'm scripting Java-based language to interface collateral MDAC kernels in real time."

"Yeah, Em-dac kernels," Buckley said. "Keep up the good work. Real time is groovy."

"It's what?"

Hands clasped behind his back like a supervisor, Buckley wandered the maze of peopled beehive cells, each having plastic nameplates identical to Stan's, though a tad smaller. He stopped when he thought he'd made a complete circuit. But there was no corner office, no familiar landmarks.

A 50-plus-year-old panic seized his throat and his lower tract. Stan quizzing him on his mom must've put the bug in his ear. He'd gotten separated from his mother in a department store. Precisely when, he couldn't remember, but it was before cars had tailfins. He was just a squirt.

Employees announced him on the p.a. and nobody came. He remembered being driven home, much much later, by them or the police. By somebody not his mom.

A young guy, half suspicious, half concerned, fingers still on his keyboard, said, "Can I help you?"

"I'm with Stan-ley Buckley and Bud Pogue," Buckley stammered.

"Are you okay, sir?"

"In the pink. I'm waiting. They're in his, Stan, Stanley's office."

"It's not easy," the kid said. "I was in Disorientation City the first six weeks I worked here, dude. Hack a left at Julie Carter's cube. Right at the tall cabinets the Captain Kirk poster's taped on, and you're home free."

Grateful and embarrassed, Buckley thanked him and reached his son's office as the two men were rising to their feet. Stan waved Buckley in.

"Sorry for the delay."

"No problem. I went exploring."

"To formalize introductions, Joe Buckley, Bud Pogue."

Buckley braced for a cruncher handshake and received one.

"Bud's caught some flak from the pool hall incident. He'll give us the details now that you're here."

"Partlow phoned our general counsel at home last night," Pogue said. "That's a fancy title for the head of our legal department. Partlow and his dipshit pals spent more energy when he was here hacking personal info than working. He alleges — sorry 'bout the lawyer word — that Mr. B attacked him physically, causing permanent injuries."

"Permanent damage? Me?"

"Nope," Pogue said. "Him. Mr. B. Mr. Buckley."

Buckley was too proud of the boy to be offended. "Well, that Partlow clown has it backasswards. He called Mr. B's brand-new bride a name. What would you do?"

"We've covered that territory," Pogue said. "I'm not disputing you guys were provoked."

"You should've seen him work over that foul-mouthed son-of-a-bitch," Buckley said, cocking his head toward his son. "Gave him a royal ass-kicking."

Pogue gave Stan a boxer's crouched feint and a playful punch to the shoulder. "Rocky Marciano reincarnated. Sonny Liston, watch out!"

Stan blushed through a full grin made lopsided by the swelling.

"The fact remains that Mr. B allegedly threw the first punch. The general counsel, who will see if he can make this thing go away not too expensively, will tend to it as soon as he's out of court today. He called me at home, asking that I debrief Mr. B. Other than the verbal abuse, were there mitigating circumstances?"

Buckley said quickly, "No allegedly about it. I advised him beforehand that if you're gonna be nailed, you throw the first punch."

"I'm not arguing you didn't impart common sense there. It won't cut no ice in this situation. We'll have to pay. Boswell is also on the bandwagon, complaining of headaches."

"Nothing wrong with him a haircut and shampoo couldn't cure," Buckley said. "A shower and an etiquette class too."

"The price will be steeper than that with him, but it better not be too steep. If Heckyl and Jeckyl want us to pay through the nose, I will interview every swinging Richard in that pool hall."

"The witnesses appeared favorable to us," Stan said.

"Witnesses tend to lose their eyesight and memories once you ask them to sign a statement or talk into a tape recorder. It depends how bad those losers want cash money in their pockets. We can build our case and drag it out in court till the cows come home. Our shyster lawyers are as nimble in that regard as anybody else's shyster lawyers."

"I outlined your difficulties," Stan told Buckley.

Buckley shrugged. "I got a few, don't I?"

"What the hey," Pogue said. "As the old saying going, life is a barrel of challenges."

Stan gestured at a desk clean but for, of course, a computer screen and a keyboard. "As you might suspect, work accumulated in my absence. I'm afraid we'll have to postpone the tour."

Buckley surmised that he meant what was happening inside the luminous box. He said no sweat and went out behind Bud Pogue. The day had been like that, him as combination kid and puppy dog, for Chrissake.

"Let's go get a cup of coffee," Pogue said to Buckley.

Bud Pogue led the way, throwing off a contrail of testosterone. The sjbWarers gave him a wide berth as they marched to the elevator and out the door. In a single motion, he unlocked a Ford Taurus, settled in, shook an unfiltered Camel out of a pack, and poised a lighter, a Zippo with a unit crest.

He asked, "You aren't one of them nicotine Nazis, are you?"

"I can roll down my window," Buckley said, doing so as Pogue started the car and his cigarette.

"That place, it can be like a fucking day care center," Pogue said. "Know what they do in there?"

"More or less," Buckley said nonchalantly. "Basically Em-dac stuff."

"Me neither. They do rake in a shitload of dough doing whatever they do and there's a spot for me cuz I understand human nature. A dinosaur like me, I won't ever be obsolete."

Cigarette firmly in mouth, Pogue floorboarded the Taurus and surged onto the highway. In the two-way turn lane he stomped on the brake pedal, then goosed it hard again to slip into traffic. Buckley's head bobbed as if mounted on a spring.

"Company car," Pogue said.

"The best kind to have on the job," Buckley said.

Not one for conversation behind the wheel, Bud Pogue drove south on a freeway. He tailgated in the carpool lane, nearly nudging the cars ahead until they moved over. Buckley braced his feet and locked his knees.

Pogue tossed his butt out as they passed a *Keep Washington Green* sign and exited. They shortcutted over a hill on residential streets and went several miles through an industrial area. He stopped at a restaurant and lounge situated between a trailer park and a machine shop. The joint had composition shingles for siding and neon beer signs in the windows. It looked to Buckley like it belonged in the neighborhood.

At this early hour there was a scattering of bleary, boozy customers at tables, watching baseball scores on an all-sports channel.

"Boeing graveyard workers just off shift," Pogue said.

"Same as you and me stopping off at four-thirty."

"You don't have to do a sales job on me."

They picked a section of the bar that had been wiped down and supplied with a clean ashtray.

"I'm killing two birds," Pogue said as they went in. "An sjbWare server worth forty grand went south last month. An inside job. There's data Mr. B's as concerned about as he is the hardware itself. A fence who's in the tech market hangs out here. I spot-check for him. Mr. B pays good wages and treats his troops right. I catch these dinks, I'll hang 'em on a fucking yardarm."

"Okay by me," Buckley said.

"What I'm doing for you is a rare occasion where Mr. B drags me away from my regular duties into something personal."

"Much appreciated."

The bartender brought Pogue a vodka on the rocks without being asked.

For an instant, Buckley thought when-in-Rome, but ordered black coffee instead.

"I see the wheels turning, Buckley," Pogue said after a drink. "You're thinking, what's this bullshit? This dump ain't a geek hangout."

"Crossed my mind."

"Classic misdirection. These nerds have IQs off the charts. A lucky tip zeroed me in here. I can hide out anywhere to take a nip."

"I suppose."

"Not that I'm hiding. I'm blending in at a surveillance location."

"Didn't say you were. Hiding, that is."

Pogue lit up and said. "The United States Army. A steadier job there never was. Three hots and a cot guaranteed. Any fool who can fog a mirror can do twenty years standing on his head and retire at fifty percent of base pay. What was your problem? What was so wrong with that? You already had seven years in."

"I'd had a bellyful."

"The Army gets a royal case of the ass when you jilt them. They become irritable beyond normal comprehension."

Tired of the patriotic lecture, Buckley asked, "You answer me a question?"

"Shoot."

"Tell me where we are. I'll call and have somebody pick me up."

Pogue downed his drink and handed the glass to the bartender. Crunching ice cubes, he said, "An attitude like that wouldn't get you far in the Army."

"It didn't."

"Or in life."

"Are we north, south, east or west of Timbuktu?" Buckley said. "Gimme a clue."

Pogue's refill came.

Coffee must be a special order here, Buckley thought. Gotta send out for a bag of grounds.

"This is Renton, where they build the 737 and 757. You walk out on me and Mr. B'll can my ass."

Buckley dismounted his barstool. "Don't worry. I'll ask him not to."

Pogue showed his palms. "All right. Sit. Here's my story. I retired as a master sergeant out of the MPs after twenty-three years in. I hauled back in more deserters than I can count. What I said to you, I had to get it off my chest. Subject closed."

Buckley sat. "Fair enough."

"You were tough as the dickens to trace, a helluva challenge."

Buckley looked at him.

"At a favor to Mr. B's mother. Eighteen years ago you

fell off the edge of the earth."

"I appreciate you solving that mystery for me, but what happened to confidentiality?"

"I'm not a priest. She knew or thought she knew you were in Belize. I'd never heard of Belize."

"Join the crowd."

"A person's relationship to other persons, while none of my concern, is impossible to avoid rubbing off on you in the investigative process. I'm what you'd call estranged myself, as they say."

"A son?"

Bud Pogue ticked them off on stumpy fingers. "Three ex-wives, two ex-sons, two ex-daughters. On Father's Day, coming up soon, I lay low, on the lookout for a hit man."

Buckley laughed at his joke, which apparently wasn't a joke. Pogue was swirling his glass, staring glumly at the booze lapping against the ice.

Buckley couldn't bring himself to say he was sorry. "In my situation, I was completely at fault. I vamoosed on them like I did the Army."

"Long-ago desertion isn't a major beef any more unless you're in the Marines," Pogue said. "The gyrenes, they'll jack you around, make sure you know the inside of a brig. The Army'll give you a discharge other than honorable. You'll have to do the interviews and the paperwork, though. It'll be like an afternoon on a ducking stool."

"I have an Oregon law firm working on my case. A Portland area outfit."

Pogue asked for a contact name and number. Buckley gave him Dotti's and watched him write it in a small pocket notebook, like the TV and movie dicks did.

"Mr. B briefed me on your fifteen minutes of fame. I got to ask, did you —?"

"Hell no. I had nothing against JFK. I've never even voted."

"I didn't think so. You were a cook, not a sniper."

"That is correct. In Basic on the rifle range, I barely qualified on the M-14."

Pogue made a pistol out of a hand and pointed at Buckley. "In a conspiracy, you don't have to be the shooter."

"You checked me out," Buckley said. "I'm a loner. Never joined a club in my life."

Bud Pogue said, "I was too young to vote then. If I had, I'd of gone for the Trickster in '60 and would've been a Goldwater man in '64."

"You and my tattoo artist."

"What frosted me more was the Cuba thing. This little country of yours, Belize, they're cozy with Fidel. They sell Cuban cigars down there, don't they?"

"I could've smuggled one up for you, hiding it where Customs wouldn't wanna look."

Pogue laughed, a sound like a car backfire. "For a guy in the middle of a shitstorm, you're a wise ass. Did that show make the regular news?"

Buckley didn't answer. It hadn't occurred to him. Pogue shook his head, went outside, and bought a newspaper in a machine. He opened it and said, "Page three. 'New JFK Probe Forthcoming?' You were a sharp-looking troop then for a cook."

Buckley looked at the photo and read a short, skeptical recap of the *Exclusive!!* episode. "Is anybody gonna take them seriously?"

"Serious enough to jack up *Exclusive!!*'s ratings. JFK conspiracy buffs are coming out of the woodwork as we speak. I'd ballpark you having two days before they catch up to you."

"Who's 'they'?"

Pogue sipped his third vodka. "Conspiracy wackos or the Fibbies. I dunno. They were tossing crumbs last night.

Tonight's show is a blockbuster if you can believe the teasing. If it was me, I'd be flying back to those tropical breezes, mucho pronto."

"I'm tempted."

"If you run for it, say goodbye to Mr. B first. He'd be hurt if you didn't. You guys had a night to remember that'd beat any bachelor party."

"I got a passport problem to clear up first."

"Your ex told Mr. B. We discussed the situation, as bizarre as it is. That's a new one on me."

"Likewise."

"It can be fixed."

"My travel agent in Belize City can also."

"Is he reliable?"

"And expensive."

"Too rich for your blood?"

"Of course not."

"Mr. B has deep pockets. They go all the way through the ground to China, they're so deep."

"No way."

"His mom?"

"I've taken advantage of gals, but never for money. That's the honest truth."

"Noble," said Bud Pogue. "You know, you're kind of reborn with a silver spoon in your mouth."

Buckley said, "None of that money is mine."

"Could've been if you and Mrs. Buckley hadn't split the sheets. She owns twenty percent of sjbWare stock."

Buckley hadn't known.

He said calmly, "sjbWare is definitely a going concern."

"On the last tally, Mr. B was ranked as the 383rd wealthiest American."

"Pretty damn good," Buckley said. "Not a billionaire, though?"

"The NASDAQ nosediving into the toilet. His net worth came in at only $645 million."

Buckley stared blankly. "Only?"

"But what the hell, when the stock market has its next orgasm, who knows."

Pogue lifted his drink.

Buckley continued waiting for his coffee.

# 13.

This had to be the goofiest experience in Joe Buckley's entire life. Had to be. It was like he was about to attend his own world premiere.

Shouldn't he be dolled up in a tux, a date with a hot-to-trot starlet lined up for afterward?

He was paying a visit to his son's mansion, not technically in it, but down a curving flight of stairs to the end of a long hall, led by Stan to his theater. All the boy lacked here was an usher's uniform and a flashlight. It occurred to Buckley that he'd never been invited into the main house proper.

Buckley had a drooling glimpse of the billiards room. Swinging saloon doors, a vintage Wurlitzer, movie posters on the wall, and a leather-pocket beauty of a table that would make Minnesota Fats swoon.

Buckley counted roughly 30 seats in the theater. Velvet curtains hung at the sides of a giant projection television. Black speakers on acoustic walls reminded him of radar air defense gizmos. There *was* a popcorn machine by the door. Buckley could go for a bag, buttered, easy on the salt, but it was empty and clean, probably there just for décor.

Beth and Susan were already seated, catty-corner, as far apart as they could and still be in the same room. A soundless nature show was on, the MUTE on the screen as big as a breadbox. Lions feasted on a large prey, leaving little to waste except the horns and hooves. Birds circling overhead, natives of darkest Africa and unknown to Buckley, were similar in size and shape to black vultures, though uglier. He related to the dead critter.

Stan told him to sit anywhere and went up to be with his bride. Lighting was low so he couldn't tell if they were dressed like twins again. Buckley sat beside Susan.

"What do you think?" she asked.

"Wow," Buckley said.

"Stanley plays Def Leppard DVD's that make the floorboards tremble."

Buckley recalled a drive-in movie, his first successful foray inside his date's blouse. This was in the days of cartoons and newsreels and double features.

Beth aimed the remote like a wand and clicked from the big kitties to Brett and Kelli, maintaining the silence. The cuties introduced a piece on a brand of vacuum cleaner that suctioned up toes as well. After this exposé of a vicious appliance, Buckley was to be the second feature, the main attraction.

They flashed an image of a grinning, gap-toothed kid, the kind of picture you could somehow tell from that he was gonna be dead or maimed. Turned out to be the latter.

Flash again to a speeding aid wagon. Hospital emergency room sign. Surgeons in gowns and masks. Some expert in a white lab coat pointing accusingly at the vacuum. Kelli, microphone in hand, hemline far north of her kneecaps, standing in front of the vacuum cleaner factory, Buckley reading "refused comment" on her moist, fire-engine-red lips.

Flash to the spunky lad in the hospital bed. Sobbing mom and grim dad. The boy's baseball coach shaking his head sadly at the lost potential. The kid on crutches, gap-toothed grin not as wide. Shot of the spunky kid's right foot, minus three toes.

Brett and Kelli doing the wrap-up.

Kelli recrossed her legs and Buckley barely noticed. Eyes misting, he was glad for the darkness. Had Stan at that age been mutilated by an attack appliance, he wouldn't've been there for him. Susan couldn't've located him to pass on the bad news either, having no Bud Pogue at her disposal back then.

Sound on now, the cuties recapped last night's guano. The sharpshooting Vietnam deserter pictured in uniform, violent criminal elements in his family, the Jack Ruby "connection", the unlikely coincidences.

"You kept that old portrait of me," Buckley said. "That's sweet."

"Shhh."

Brett gazed earnestly at his audience. "Our source of this disturbing information, who we shall refer to as Mister A is with us tonight in the studio for an exclusive interview."

Kelli said, "Mister A has agreed to answer questions, providing that we disguise his voice and appearance."

"Mr. A for Mr. Asshole," Buckley muttered.

"A courageous act irregardless," Brett said. "True, this information has come to light very recently and it's circumstantial at best, but if there's any validity whatsoever in the allegations, Mr. A may be in jeopardy."

Kelli shuddered provocatively.

"His life wouldn't be worth a plug nickel," Brett added.

"The information, ironically, comes from a source quite intimate to Private First Class Joseph Buckley," Kelli said, pausing for effect. "His lover."

"Pillow talk is often the most revealing," Brett said, nodding vigorously.

"We'll refer to her as Madame X, a former companion of PFC Buckley. In fact, Mister A has steadfastly refused to divulge her identity, in order to protect her. We can assume she is still alive and also be in potential peril."

"Chivalry ain't dead," Buckley whispered.

"Mr. A has courageously agreed to read verbatim from

the incriminating documents, Kelli."

"A meticulously detailed journal, Brett."

"What the hell?" Susan said so loudly that Beth and Stanley turned around.

Andrew's outline, in all its pencil-necked glory, appeared, a head-on view, black on a white background. Holding a book at his side, he looked like an alien in a low budget sci-fi flick.

"Mister A promises that Madame X reveals her innermost feelings in her own words," Kelli said. "This material may be unsuitable for younger viewers."

"He wouldn't stoop *that* low," Susan said. "He wouldn't."

Andrew began, elbows out, a whooping crane silhouette. His voice was Elmer Fudd's after too much caffeine.

"I awoke to a glorious dawn cascading through the window, its morning hue casting golden highlights on Joe's sinewy arm as we lay entwined, spent and exhausted after a night –"

"Stanley, please mute this for a second?"

Beth took the remote from her husband and did, restoring the sound with –

"– the oddly bizarre headless eagle, his one and only tattoo. Dear Diary, don't ask me how I know! I cannot tell a lie! It's sad, sad origin, imprinted as it was on his arm while President Kennedy's motorcade traveled inexorably to its horrific fate."

"In exor-what?" Buckley said.

"Oh God," Susan said. "The lousy bleeping bleep."

"Then he awakened and I happily succumbed again to his insatiable desire, moving together in a pagan rhythm, uttering incoherent moans of pleasure."

"This is so embarrassing," she said into Buckley's shoulder.

Buckley was embarrassed for Susan too, and for himself, for being aroused in mixed company.

"We showered together interminably, gloriously and languidly, uncaring when the hot water was depleted, so fiercely did our internal furnaces burn."

Stan's pager beeped. He hurried out a side door underneath an authentic green EXIT sign. At least he kept it in a pocket, not on his belt, gunslinger style, like everybody and their brother did with their beepers and phones in this day and age.

Brett broke in. "We'll return for the remainder of Madame X's startling revelations after these messages."

Insatiable, Buckley thought. An important reason their marriage failed was that he'd become semi-uninsatiable at home, while being satiable elsewhere. Of the multitude of dumb-ass stunts he'd pulled in his life, him losing Susan rated in the top five.

Susan had slipped out of the theater. Her and her romance novels, Buckley thought. She could write her own, word for word, right out of her diaries. Corner the market.

Stan returned and spoke to Beth. Whatever it was, he seemed relieved.

Kelli and Brett mopped up by saying that history might have to be the judge. No corroboration had been provided on the secret society based on the headless eagle tattoo.

"A decapitated eagle," Kelli said, shivering furtively. "The symbolism gives me the creeps. It's, it's anti-American."

"Private First Class Joe Buckley," Brett said, pointing a finger at the camera.

Buckley almost answered.

"Joseph J. Buckley, wherever you are, Mister A states that you are home from your misguided exile. He cannot or will not corroborate his statement, but if it is accurate, I implore you to do the right thing for yourself and your country. If you have information that can finally bring closure to the incident that decimated the Kennedy family, you have an obligation to come forward. Telephone the nearest FBI office and turn yourself in. Tell what you know and make your peace with your nation, the United States Army, and your conscience."

After Beth buzzed in his ear, Stan cut out the side exit again. Buckley was giving Brett the finger when Beth turned Brett off, turned the lights on, and turned around.

"Mr. Buckley, do you have a minute?"

"You betcha. Call me Joe."

They met halfway on a carpeted aisle, which had those tiny, little floor lights, same as a real theater.

"I want to thank you for being there for my husband last night. Him defending my honor, that was endearing."

Buckley replied with an aw-shucks shrug.

"We have some good news. Stanley's page was from our corporate counsel. He's settled with Partlow and Boswell. The agreement stipulates a gag order. They cannot take their story to the media."

"Well, yeah, that is good news."

"And thank you for the antique bicycle," she said quickly, getting an unpleasant topic out of her system. "We certainly enjoyed it."

"You're certainly welcome."

"Stanley didn't have a conventional bachelor party. Your outing, the drinking and brawling, it was a memorable substitute for him."

"Trust me when I say that the situation wasn't our intention, his or mine."

"However. You were there, not at the airport, your original destination."

Beth had a severe dose of what they called body

language. She'd folded her arms as tight as duct tape and her smile was frozen.

"It was my idea," Buckley lied. "I insisted. We stopped off for pizza and beer. A person has to eat."

"I've asked Stanley to see a doctor concerning his injury."

"It's looking better," Buckley said.

"He's procrastinating. I'm worried about infection."

Buckley prudently did not mention Susan's antibiotic ointment treatment. He did not say that the boy's fat lip would be fine in a day or two, that it was a whole different ball game than the vacuum cleaner kid on *Exclusive!!*"

"Yeah, I'm with you. A checkup wouldn't hurt."

Beth tapped her own lip. "He could be left with a scar."

"Yeah, he might."

"Stanley assured me that the allegations on that trashy show are totally false. Andrew Cardigan is simply in a jealous rage. You and, well, Mrs. Buckley on our wedding night. We heard."

Buckley didn't comment.

"Stanley finds your side of the family intriguing, as I'm sure you're aware."

"Oh yeah, I am aware."

"I didn't know until we began making wedding arrangements. His interest, frankly, is bordering on the macabre. No disrespect intended, but his attraction is the less positive aspects of your family, centered on your late brother. I assume these elements are not especially a matter of pride to you."

"I've tried to play down his Uncle Stan. He wasn't Baby Face Nelson. He was the world's most inept bank robber."

"However. You do have issues."

"Issues?"

"Significant issues, beginning with the U.S. Army."

"Oh that. I have an important Portland attorney on the case."

"What are your plans, may I ask?"

"Plans," Buckley said. "Well, I'm considering several alternatives."

"As unjust as that President Kennedy conspiracy madness is, there will be unwanted attention. It's inevitable, a matter of time before they track you down. I hope you sue that imbecilic show out of business. In the meantime, if you are here with us, it logically follows that the search and the attention will culminate here with us."

Sue the bastards? Buckley mentally snapped his fingers.

"No sweat. I'll leave whenever you say the word."

"You're welcome to stay indefinitely, Mr. Buckley. Our resources and those of the company are at your disposal."

"Thanks, but I'll be out of your hair soon."

"You are, well, family. I'm merely addressing the possible ramifications. Stanley is a significant member of the high-tech and corporate community. He has a reputation, a standing. We have future philanthropic aspirations."

"You two kids have done good for yourselves. I'm very proud."

"However. When I say indefinitely, are you aware that Stanley's mother is in the market for a condo?"

"Yep."

"A real estate broker friend has shown her properties she's attracted to. A downtown penthouse and an equally spacious unit in a gorgeous lakeside complex. They're new construction, available immediately, as soon as she decides."

"Terrific."

"We'll be making other uses of the coach house. My mother will be moving in."

"Irene will love the place," Buckley said. "Is she a birder?"

"A bird watcher? No."

"Too bad. You've got waterfowl galore. In the shoreline snags, she could expect bald eagles. If she's lucky, a pileated woodpecker."

"My mother is ambivalent about living here, but she doesn't have the resources to be too flexible."

Beth was tightening her grip on herself. Buckley was afraid she'd snap a rib. He admired her protective attitude. Like a mother bird, she'd peck your eyeballs out if you threatened her family.

"You don't have to explain to me."

"My father is experiencing a second adolescence, at my mother's emotional and financial expense."

"I understand."

"My father has an MBA and was a middle manager at Boeing. Heather was a hair stylist. What can they talk about, what can they have in common?"

Buckley wasn't gonna touch that one with a 10-foot pole. Not a 10,000-foot pole. He said nothing.

"Father took an early retirement he couldn't afford to take to play house," she continued. "He feels my mother's settlement demands are intransigent and unreasonable. What she has coming is tied up in legal squabbling."

"Lawyers," Buckley said, rolling his eyes.

"I love my father. You can't help but to love a wayward parent, never mind what they have done or not done to you and for you in the past or present."

Ouch, Buckley thought.

"Middle-aged men have a propensity for cutting a swath through lives."

"I suppose some do. Sure."

"So much has happened so fast to Stanley. It's difficult for anyone to absorb and maintain an even keel."

"Uh huh," Buckley said. "Absolutely."

"I'm discovering that Stanley is surprisingly impressionable. Arrested adolescent behavior, if I may be blunt, is an unhealthy influence."

"Ouch," Buckley said.

"I didn't mean you. Not in that regard."

"Okay. Not being 'it' is nice for a change."

"I meant my father. You operate a restaurant. You continue to lead a productive life. You have responsibilities and you face them."

"Yes," Buckley said, his memory suddenly jogged. "Yes I do."

# 14.

"Molly's."

"Hey Keith, is that you?"

"Yeah, who's this?"

"How come you're answering the phone?"

"I'm sitting down beside the phone drinking a Belikin and it rang. Who's this?"

"Buckley."

"Who?"

"Joe Buckley."

"Who?"

"Joe Buckley. I own Molly's."

"Yeah? Where you at?"

"Up in the States."

"Yeah? How come?"

"My son's wedding. I told you."

"No you didn't."

"Yeah, I did. Remember my boy's letter, the paralleobox around his company logo. I showed you that letter."

"Now I remember. You at the wedding?"

"No, the wedding's over."

"How come you ain't back in San Ignacio if the wedding's over?"

"Long story. I'll be home soon. How's Molly's doing?"

"You better talk to the boss lady."

"The boss lady."

"Yeah. Lady who you're lucky you're a million miles from right now."

"Sharon? Sharon Usher?"

"That's her."

"Is she there?"

"You're in some hot water."

"Keith."

"Hello."

"Sharon. Is that you?"

"Joe Buckley?"

"Sharon, how you doing? How come you're answering the phone?"

Silence.

"Sharon, you still there?"

"Is this the man who promised to keep in constant touch?"

"It's good to hear the sound of your voice too."

More silence.

"I've had complications you wouldn't believe. Issues. Up here in the States, anything that goes haywire, they call it an issue. Issues. That's what they call them."

"No, I don't guess I would believe."

"For openers, some thief stole my luggage and all my belongings."

"That's what you say."

"It's the honest truth, Sharon."

"When are you coming back?"

"Pretty soon. So how's Molly's Restaurant running? I hear people in the background, I hear kitchen sounds. Lots of customers?"

"Molly's is running into the open arms of its new owners."

"Huh?"

"Two nice fellows just retired out of the British army. Responsible, earnest, hard working fellows. They will be here working every single, solitary day."

"Let's not do anything rash."

"Eighteen hours a day working two jobs is not rash,

Buckley. You forgot to replace yourself and you forgot to pay a cook who quit on me."

"I'll be home before you know it, Sharon. Hang in there."

"The deal is made. They are coming in the morning to sign the papers."

Silence.

"Buckley, you there?"

"Okay, Sharon, I guess you gotta do what you gotta do. What's my cut?"

Click.

Dial tone.

# 15.

The time: zero dark thirty.

Windows opened wide, Joe Buckley sat by his bed, eyes and ears attuned until he could no longer see or hear anything. Not actually *not anything*.

The occasional bird tune (American robin and song sparrow and red-winged blackbird) and a slight rustling breeze, sure.

No *whoopa-whoopa-whoopa* of helicopter blades, though. No metallic clicking by a SWAT team locking and loading, either. No bullhorns, no slick-talking negotiation experts telephoning him. No conspiracy nutcases grappling up the wall.

Not yet. It was just him, all by his lonesome, him and his paranoia.

Thanks to the twilight, it wasn't really pitch-black dark. Buckley remembered summer twilight from his Oregon childhood. In tropical Belize there were 12 hours of darkness and 12 hours daylight year-round, give or take an hour. When the sun set it was as if somebody had dropped a bucket over it.

Up in the Pacific Northwest's latitude, this near the summer solstice, you had sixteen hours of daylight. At nighttime, ol' Sol appeared to burrow barely six inches underneath the horizon.

Buckley's non-paranoiac concern was activity within the Stanley J. Buckley estate. Not a soul was stirring. He had already packed, so he tiptoed out, gently closing his door. He'd written a note too, and rewritten it and rewritten it. In an oddly formal tone, Buckley thanked everybody for everything.

While he knew he sounded stupid and phony, like an Oscar winner accepting the little gold statue, he still didn't have a handle who he was to anybody. In a nutshell, he apologized for slinking away, but desired as soon as possible to spare innocent parties the stigma and complications of harboring Public Enemy Number One. Try as he might, he couldn't hear his own voice in that piece of paper.

He reviewed the PS the hardest.

*PS: I hope it is okay that I borrow the Corvette and promise to call saying where I drop it off, which will be in a safe and secure spot. I apologize for inconveniences I caused and if this ISN'T okay, please give me a day before reporting the vehicle stolen. Love, Joe.*

What he was doing, he told himself, he was being proactive. He was turning over a new leaf. No more procrastination for Joe Buckley, no more sticking to his motto of never putting off till tomorrow what you can do next week, maybe.

He rationalized that he was not stealing the car. He wasn't even sneaking out in it for the evening in another weird father-son role flip-flop, like Wally and the Beaver poaching Ward's car keys out of his pocket while he snoozed through *I Love Lucy*. He was doing the family a favor. Nobody would be forced into the position of feeling that they had to bestow further undeserved charity on him.

Bud Pogue had told Buckley that he was in the middle of a shitstorm. Truer words were never spoken. By bugging out, Buckley was dragging that thick, brown cloud along with him.

He hesitated at Susan's door, listening. Nary a peep. For the tenth time, he almost knocked. But when she was that red-faced following a situation, she preferred being left to herself. Stan had been by shortly after *Exclusive!!*.

Buckley heard her door shut, then saw him walking to the main house later, bless his heart. A good boy to attempt to comfort her, a damn good boy.

He slipped the note under her door and, rising to his feet, noticed something different. All that remained of Andrew's picture was a nail hole in the wall.

He went downstairs, unhooked the power door mechanism in the Corvette's bay and ever so carefully rolled it up by hand. He spotted *The View from Wherever* leaning between garbage cans. Buckley tossed it in the car, it being trash of no further value to this particular household. Maybe he could pawn it for a few bucks. There'd at least be a piddling payback for the JFK guano.

Buckley pushed the Vette as far from the main house as he could before starting the engine. Idling, it rumbled like jungle drums. He eased up the drive and out onto the road, gave it the gas, and fishtailed into a shallow ditch. It occurred to him that it had been years since he'd driven a car, let alone a hot rod.

Where to next?

The story of his life lately.

Careful on the gas this time, Buckley pulled up onto the shoulder, stopped, and dug a map out of the glove box. He could go straight to the airport. The Vette would be safe in their parking garage.

Or.

The map covered Oregon and Washington. He could make Portland before dawn, spruce up at a motel and see Dotti. He was, after all, a man without a country with no old-age security to go home to, and as Andrew had tagged him, an international fugitive.

Let's get the legal process moving.

Buckley picked up *The View from Whichever*. He'd draw a mustache on the thing if he could locate a logical place to draw it. Maybe he'd stop on the bridge and chuck it into Lake Washington, a raft for the seagulls. A trademark Buckley gesture, he knew. Immature as it was, he'd feel better, and any warm feeling at the moment was welcome.

He looked on the back of the canvas at a rubber-stamping with Andrew Cardigan's name and address. He circled the address on the map and decided to take a detour. What he'd do, he didn't exactly know. He was leaning toward tearing the canvas out of the frame, folding and stuffing it in Andrew's mail slot, waiting for him when he returned from LA. After scribbling a good-bye note and his John Hancock on the back.

He didn't want Susan blamed for the stunt. He definitely wanted all the credit himself.

Buckley had wronged him, yeah, but Andrew had gotten even in spades, particularly to Susan. Buckley flexed his fists. They weren't hurting and he could hardly see the wedding night scrapes. Buckley did not intend to go to the artist's looking for that sort of trouble, but if Andrew was in the market for a knuckle sandwich, he was ready, willing and able to serve one up with all the trimmings.

Fifteen minutes later, he was on the bridge smiling.

Typical Buckley, Susan would say.

Classic Joe Buckley.

No point growing up at this stage of the game, no use wringing your hands over the life you'd pissed away. Fuck that. How many hundreds of times had Sooz told him that he was having the childhood he had been deprived of as a child? Those old hippie expats he held in such contempt, all he had on them was a haircut.

Then he had to go and start crying for no reason. Bawling like a fucking baby. Over his own woes, over his half-assed fall into age-60 geezerhood, over the Corvette reminding him of dead Dave Kenworthy? He hadn't the foggiest. He pulled his shirt up to wipe his eyes on. No taillights in sight. He tromped on the accelerator and upshifted, printing tread on the deck.

At mid-span, Buckley clocked a blurry speed limit sign: 50. Belize had no speed limits. He gripped the wheel in a hurricane, the speedometer needle quivering at 125. At the western high rise, the car left the ground. He stepped off the gas. The Vette landed on all fours, *kerthump,* like a big cat, steady as she goes.

Buckley wasn't suicide crazy, eager to fly off into the drink or to be chased down by traffic cops who'd have their holsters unsnapped. His ticker hammering his chest told him that much.

Calming down, Buckley meandered south of downtown Seattle, by two new stadiums, one for baseball, the other for football under construction, money being no object up here in the States. The plants and shops and storage yards south of the ballparks were the machinery of the city, Buckley thought, doing the hard dirty work that hadn't already been farmed out to countries such as Honduras and Bangladesh and Red China.

Andrew lived in a non-neighborhood of loading docks and smokestacks. Railroad tracks ran parallel to the main drag. Graveyard shifts worked behind sooty glass and warehouses seemed to extend a mile deep. He passed a windowless barroom, pickups and motorcycles lined up outside, a dive that Joe Buckley in his brawling prime might not have avoided.

Balloons had gotten loose from a used car lot full of clunkers. Some had shriveled. They hung by their strings on cars like spoiled fruit. Others bobbed on the pavement. Buckley slalomed through them for the fun of it.

When he reached Andrew's general area, he'd pretty much gotten hold of himself. Gals he'd known were unanimous that you always felt restored after a good, wet, rousing, for-no-particular-reason cry. Although he'd never ever admit his breakdown to a single soul, Buckley tended to agree.

The sheer dumbness of his intentions finally smacked him in the chops. On a side street, he stopped to consult his map and to a flip a coin. To hell with Andrew and his picture.

Heads, Seattle-Tacoma International Airport.

Not as Harold Roy Qwerty. Who the hell was he kidding?

Tails, Portland and the law offices of Cline, Sedgwick, Holmes and Magnuson.

If it landed on end, and the way his situation was going, he wouldn't bet against it, he'd surrender to the authorities.

Parked, coin on thumb to be launched, he happened to look at the street signs. There it was, by God, right on the corner, Andrew's home sweet home, his studio or loft, LEATHER GOODS in old-timey lettering in faded white on a side of an old brick building. Some of the tenants used newspaper for curtains.

Andrew's kind of pad. Buckley checked the mailboxes for his unit and found it. He walked up the steps with the artwork, having decided he'd lean it on Andrew's door unharmed, just as he'd found it by the garbage cans. Kelli and Brett would say that was ironic, that it'd decimate Andrew's ego.

If he'd carried out his original plan, besides being an Army-deserting traitor and Cuba-loving, co-conspiring, political maniac, he'd be an art vandal and thief, absconding with a masterpiece. Playing it cool like this, Andrew would get the picture in more ways than one. Susan would approve.

It was slow going. The stairs were loose and creaky. Two out of three overhead light bulbs were missing, no doubt requisitioned by the starving artists. Andrew's hallway was completely unlighted. Nary a sliver beamed from his unit or his neighbors.

Buckley rested *The View from Whoever* against Andrew's door and turned to leave.

The door moved inward a crack.

Must be ajar, nudged by the weight of picture frame and canvas and wasted paint. Inside lights were out. He stuck his head through and watched the silhouette millions of TV viewers now recognized. It was doing what Buckley had considered doing to *Whoever*, removing canvases from frames.

Except Andrew was lovingly rolling and taping them, instead of angrily folding them into halves and quarters.

Buckley cleared his throat.

Andrew turned in a slow-motion crouch. "Who's there?"

"Lee Harvey Oswald to you, Mr. A for Asshole."

# 16.

This had to be the second goofiest experience in Joe Buckley's entire life. Had to be. Himself in the doorway, Andrew Cardigan in his crouch, clutching a rolled-up masterpiece like a club. By all rights, both should be thousands of miles from Seattle, but there they were, staring each other down in whatever crummy streetlight that managed to slip in through the windows.

"How'd Mister A zoom home so fast?"

"The show was taped this afternoon."

"Not real time, huh?"

"I caught the earliest available flight. What are you doing here as opposed to your tropical hideaway?"

"I had travel issues. Going on another trip?"

"Not by choice."

After 30 seconds tops, the tension had swirled out of the encounter like bathwater down a drain. Cool as you please, Andrew said have a seat and would he like a drink.

Buckley said sure to the drink, unclenched his fists, felt his way inside, and swooshed into a beanbag chair.

No point making a bad situation worse by butting antlers, he thought. Andrew was in some jackpot of his own. Their calmness was male intuition, instinctive self-preservation. There was no territory to defend and they were floating up separate branches of Shit Creek without paddles, both in leaky kayaks.

Andrew shut the door. He lit a candle that'd been stuck in a Chianti bottle on a wooden barrel that did duty as a coffee table, then poured screw-top jug wine into paper cups. The apartment-studio was one large room that reeked of turpentine. Even in the dark, Buckley could tell it had higher ceilings than Stan's home theater and that it was a dump.

In jeans, plain white T-shirt, and hairy as Tarzan's Cheetah, Andrew was a homely Tinkertoy. With a shudder of revulsion, he imagined Andrew climbing into Susan's bed and atop its occupant.

"Permit me to extend my apologies for the televised tabloid fiasco," Andrew said.

"Hey," Buckley said, lifting a shoulder. "Forget it. Water under the bridge."

"At the wedding, you hurt me. Badly."

Buckley squinted, scanning for injuries. Wherever the blood had come from, he'd healed. "I apologize for my part in our scuffle. I'll pay your doctor bills, Andrew. No sweat."

"I meant you plural, you and Susan, emotionally and psychologically. How long since you had been together?"

"A while."

"Not an hour transpired before you two became a couple again, reliving your passion."

Andrew was a sad-eyed basset hound.

"We'd had a few drinks. That wine punch, wow, was it ever sneaky!"

"Just that quickly, the relationship Susan and I built over of nearly two years dissolved. I was out of her life."

"Nah. C'mon, think of her and me on the beach as auld lang syne. If we still had the mutual hots, we wouldn't be living three thousand miles apart."

"I responded to the threat of your intimacy with inappropriate language and precipitated a physical confrontation. I cannot condone my behavior."

Andrew was yakking like some mope in Susan's romance novels, the guy aced out for the girl by the pirate. Buckley wanted to put an end to this. "Andrew, Sooz and me, we're friends is all. We had a kid together. When we were dancing, I don't recall us being too far out of line."

"I'll grant that your dancing style was subjective."

Between his ears, Buckley heard the Righteous Brothers and *Unchained Melody*. He resisted humming.

"That's right. There you go. The dirty boogie to one person is an accidentally lively dance sequence on account of strong drink and the inspiration of a particular tune."

"When I left the reception, I did not see you or Susan."

"All we did was walk along the beach and talk. I swear on a stack of Bibles," Buckley lied, raising his right hand. "Absolutely, positively nothing happened between us. We were strictly platonical."

Andrew looked at him. He wasn't buying it.

Quickly changing the subject, Buckley said, "Not to belabor our rumpus too much, did I actually injure you?"

"Stop worrying. I hardly felt your blows."

Buckley tapped his chin. "Go ahead and take a free poke if you believe I owe you."

"No, no, no. I slipped in the sand and cut myself on a broken sand dollar. It was nothing."

"It was?" Buckley contained his disappointment. "Okay, well, good."

"I craved vengeance. I committed an inexcusably spiteful act by stealing Susan's diaries."

"A felony is what it is if you wanna split hairs, which I'm not doing."

"I knew your background in general terms. That diary was a wealth of specifics. The episode I recited on camera was heartbreakingly titillating."

Among other episodes, Buckley fondly remembered.

"Hey, listen, so you beelined right to *Exclusive!!*." He waved his arms in conciliation. "I'd've done the very same thing. They must pay a bundle."

"I didn't contact them initially. I notified every law enforcement agency in the telephone directory blue pages, from city police departments to the county sheriff to the state patrol to provost marshal offices of local military posts to the United States Attorney to the FBI. Nobody demonstrated the slightest interest in a Vietnam-era deserter."

Buckley coughed on a swallow of wine and slapped himself on the chest. "They weren't? They didn't?"

"I had no takers, none whatsoever. In typically bureaucratic fashion, they passed the buck and handed me off to somebody else until I was dizzy from going around in circles. If you were a spy or wanted for a serious crime or if your desertion hadn't taken place over a third of a century ago, it would be different. Bottom line, you represented a paperwork bother, no more, no less. You were not in their criminal records and you were no Rambo-esque menace to society."

Though skeptical, Buckley said, "Yeah. I was a cook."

"Who in candor did not extinguish a single human life in Vietnam?"

"Lots of guys didn't, Andrew. A small fraction of GI's in my day there were grunts paddy-humping for Charlie. Even at the height of the build-up, they say like one in seventeen was a grunt. The rest were cooks and paper shufflers and such.

"I got no VC scalps to my credit. In the Tan Son Nhut mess hall, we'd sometimes forgot and left stuff sitting out that should be in the cooler, so who knows about friendly casualties." Buckley snapped his fingers. "In Saigon's climate, food can spoil like that. Mayo turns as deadly as nerve gas."

"My inspiration came in a moment of meanness and greed. I saw *Exclusive!!* recently when they featured transvestite venereal disease and an Amelia Earhart sighting, although I don't as a rule watch trash television."

"Sounds like a fun episode."

"I was eager to learn the secrets Susan's diaries held. When I left the coach house, they came along with a framed photo of you she had in the box in which she kept her old diaries. It made me doubly jealous. How I envied you, Joe."

If I go to the grave with anything I'm proud of, Buckley thought, it's that I never ever peeked inside Sooz's private pages. "Yeah, well, we'd best lay the subject to rest."

"Agreed," Andrew said. "The chapter about you in Dallas and your tattoo struck a chord. I noticed the headless eagle after the wedding as Susan was examining it. Very unusual."

"It definitely is a conversation piece," Buckley said.

"I was born on November 22, 1963. This, in these circumstances, was fate, karma, destiny, kismet. Temptation overwhelmed me."

"Susan told me about your date of birth. Maybe you were Lee Harvey Oswald's love child, huh?"

Unsmiling, possessing no sense of humor, Andrew freshened their paper cups. "I emerged from the womb at twelve-thirty in the afternoon. You are aware of the historical significance."

"Yeah. It wasn't too much later that my tattooer switched off his needle and went outside to check on the commotion."

"I love a conspiracy as much as the next individual, but my exhaustive research precludes a scenario that does not place Lee Harvey Oswald as the lone gunman, a disturbed individual taking the ultimate advantage of time and placement."

"You couldn't tell that from Brett and Kelli."

"Sounding as mysterious as possible, I contacted *Exclusive!!* and said I had a document and a photo."

"Document as in diary?"

"They loved the word 'document'. They accepted my

presentation and bought me an airline ticket to Los Angeles."

"How is that little Kelli close up?" Buckley asked.

"As tough as Sheffield steel and thirty-five if she's a day. High-definition television is going to end careers like talkies did. Brett should have half her gumption. When the producer admonished him for saying 'irregardless' on the air, he cried."

Wondering why the producer made a federal case out of "irregardless", Buckley said, "So they swallowed your story without backup proof?"

"Initially. JFK conspiracy theories remain irresistible. *Exclusive!!* pressed me for more substantive facts today prior to the show. I think the bigwigs had a disagreement whether to utilize me or not. That's why I think they stalled on my check."

"You were being paid how much?"

"I was promised fifty thousand dollars."

Buckley whistled. "Fifty grand. What's my share?"

"I was waiting on my money. The producer said they were cutting the check in the bookkeeping office. He said he'd personally wait until it was ready and for me to stay put. He was acting fishy. I slipped out a side door with the diaries and your photo when he left the room. In a no-parking slot I spotted a plain white sedan and its occupants."

"Uh oh. Detectives?"

"FBI is my guess. Two men in civilian clothes had crew cuts and wallet badges folded over their jacket pockets. They were embroiled in an intense conversation with the producer. *Exclusive!!* won outstanding ratings, then did their duty, cheating me out of my money in the process."

"You oughta sue the bastards. I may do so myself for slander. I've got me a damn good lawyer down in Portland," Buckley said.

"You have my blessing."

"Aren't you afraid the Feds are gonna storm in on you?"

"I gave *Exclusive!!* a fictitious address. I presume they have subsequently discovered the truth."

"I oughta be running along so you can finish your packing," Buckley said.

"Not to worry. I have a comfortable head start."

"Famous last words. Can I ask you a question, Andrew, about you and Susan?"

"You may ask."

Buckley hadn't asked another guy how he felt about a girl since the sixth grade. He fidgeted, trying to bring forth the words.

"The true nature of my affection for her?"

"You got it."

"My feelings for her are so incredibly complex I cannot begin to sort them out so soon after our breakup."

"She was that Peggy Googlyeyes person to you?"

Andrew gave him a condescending smirk. "Susan did make the accusatory Peggy Guggenheim-Jackson Pollock analogy more than once."

Buckley didn't reply.

"Susan is financially secure."

"Financially secure? She's loaded," Buckley said. "I guess she's got greenbacks coming out her ears."

"I am aware of that. We lived at her son's new home for six months and here seven months earlier. Thanks to sjbWare, Her wealth increased exponentially in that period. When she was awarded stock in her son's IPO, it didn't change her. I cannot say the same for me. In retrospect, our relationship subtly evolved in inverse proportion from lovers to patron-artist."

"You popped the question the other day?"

"What is a successful marriage if not a partnership?

I'm at a crossroads in my career. I'm over forty years of age, no *enfant terrible* or *wunderkind* by any stretch, with a career total of eleven thousand dollars in sales. Am I a community college art instructor and hobbyist or a serious painter?

Andrew gestured at the pile of rolled-up paintings that made Buckley think of the Dead Sea Scrolls set for recycling.

"My ego brought me back here. I cannot go underground without my life's work. Incidentally, why are you here?"

"I'm returning your picture from Susan's. It's out by your door."

Andrew leaned forward, elbows on knees. "Painting, not picture. Susan asked you to return *Trieste*? It was a very special gift from me to her, our pre-engagement present."

Jesus, Andrew was more concerned about his artwork being dumped than himself. Buckley supposed that went with the ego territory necessary to sign your name on a canvas you'd slopped paint on. But he couldn't twist the dagger in the Tinkertoy, just couldn't.

"Nah. I sort of took the errand upon myself. Sooz is in the market for a condo and she's sort of thinning things out."

"In any event, thank you for returning *Trieste*."

"No problem."

"I'm attempting to fathom your role in our lives, Mr. Buckley."

"Me too. I came to a wedding and the situation took on a life of its own."

"Susan said she persuaded her son to invite you as a courtesy. It was his birthday and wedding day, and Father's Day was upcoming. She was not confident you would attend."

Buckley held out his cup. "Me neither. But here I am."

Andrew poured a generous refill.

"Mighty smooth bouquet to this stuff."

Andrew touched Buckley's cup in toast, not spilling much when the soggy cardboard bent. "Are you an art lover?"

"I'm an art liker."

"Your favorites?"

"I'm partial to Norman Rockwell and John James Audubon."

Andrew gave the ceiling a Lord-help-me look.

Buckley said, "We have a bunch of fine artists in Belize?"

"Painters? Sculptors?"

"You name it, they do it."

"Abstract expressionists?"

"I don't know. Much of their stuff is of people and what you find in nature. They're fairly good and they sell primarily to tourists, selling them what they like to buy."

"There isn't a great deal of nonrepresentational work in your country?"

"If you mean you can't tell what it is, I guess we have our share of that. I'm not always sure that's what the artist intended when he started out. I considered setting up a corner of my restaurant as a gift shop, selling arts and crafts."

"How is your restaurant doing in your absence?"

"Not as well as I'd hoped." Buckley decided to perk Andrew up with a little white lie. "In fact, your stuff would be a big hit at Molly's."

"It would?"

Buckley's eyes had adjusted enough to appraise pictures still leaning and hanging on the wall behind Andrew. He thought of one as *Paintball Firing Squad* and another *Grape Stomp Residue in Yesterday's Cornflakes*.

"You betcha. The various colors you dab on, people buy art for décor, you know, to match what they go in their homes. You have something for everybody."

Andrew Cardigan began to speak, but a response would not escape.

"I really oughta get going," Buckley said.

"Please finish your wine. There's no hurry."

Buckley looked at him. "What's going on?"

"Pardon me?"

"You should be jumping through hoops to throw your gear together and be out the door."

Andrew refilled the wine cups.

"Where are you gonna lay low, if I may ask?"

"I have a confession."

"Don't we all."

"Destination Nowhere. You arrived when my flight charade was almost completed. The paintings I'll rolled up are lesser works."

"Bingo. You gave the Feds a lightweight challenge with the fake address by bugging out of the studio and whetted their appetites besides."

"Guilty as charged."

"That's why you didn't lock the door."

"I have a damage deposit I cannot afford to forfeit," Andrew said.

"Yeah, a battering ram and tear gas and assault weapon bullets tend to be messy."

"Fleeing was a spontaneous decision. I had an epiphany," Andrew said. "I truly was frightened. On the plane, I began to analyze my plight and came to the conclusion I didn't have a plight. I had sold *Exclusive!!* innuendo and speculation and they bought it. I was not misrepresenting the material and I had no knowledge of a conspiracy."

"They catch you here, hassle you some, and you get

what for your trouble, an encore on that show?"

"Notoriety," Andrew said, winking.

"I gotcha," Buckley said, raising his cup. "Artists usually have to be dead before their sales take off. This kind of publicity is even better for your career than dying."

Andrew pointed at a canvas on the wall. "What do you see when you absorb that piece?"

Absorb? A mishmash of slashes in hump patterns, sort of. "A very pretty picture, Andrew."

"Painting! The title is *Carpathian Equinox*. I'm renaming it *Dallas Denouement*."

"Hey, that'll work. Go with what's hot."

"And that canvas on the easel."

Buckley interpreted a pile of old tires on fire in a diseased orchard.

"A work in progress."

"Sure. Obviously."

"*Dealey Disintegration*. It may become my *Guernica*."

"Don't see why not, Andrew. Hey, the sky's the limit."

Andrew again topped off Buckley's cup.

"Lemme guess. You're cozying up to me on account it takes two to tango or conspire. The gendarmes come and haul us off. They keep me and turn you loose. You make the papers, sell a ton of pictures, and live happily ever after."

"The wine's on me and the risk is low of your arrest is extremely low."

"Says you." Joe Buckley was prepared to leave, damn weary of co-conspiracies, but his posterior could not escape the beanbag. So they settled in for a night of cheap wine and waiting and lightweight conversation.

# 17.

Joe Buckley awakened to Andrew puttering about, tugging on and slamming sticky cabinet doors, banging and clanking silverware and plates. Women he had lived with made similar statements when angry. Andrew Cardigan was just clumsy.

Buckley blearily focused on the kitchen area. It consisted of a sink, a half-size fridge, and a toaster and a hotplate connected to a fire hazard lash-up of extension cords.

Car dealer ads and the comic strips served as drapes on Andrew's high windows. They were taped on curtain rods and glowed in the direct morning sun like cathedral stained glass, Toyotas and cartoon dogs instead of angels.

Starving artist economics or an artsy-fartsy statement? Buckley hadn't the foggiest and cared not to inquire.

"Breakfast?" Andrew asked. "Coffee's on."

Buckley shivered. "Please. Can we turn the heat on too?"

Bending over the counter, pouring coffee, Andrew looked to Buckley like a praying mantis. "In June?"

"Me and my thin blood, I'm in the Great White North amongst Eskimos."

He took a mug from Andrew, blew on the steam, and said, "Thanks. No police raid, huh?"

"No raid." Andrew glanced between funny pages. "I've been watching constantly since pre dawn. Raids historically are staged at dawn."

In the movies they are, Buckley didn't say.

Victor Charles mortared Dave Kenworthy in mid-morning.

Andrew's and his raids, he was a bit too much of an

eager beaver to suit Buckley. The prospect of scared, pissed-off law enforcement folk with flak vests and guns crashing in on them did not appeal.

Molded into the beanbag chair where he'd dozed off, Buckley sipped coffee as he watched his host drop slices of bread as dry and hard as toast into the toaster.

Buckley needed to climb back on his proactivated horse and get the hell out of here. He figured he'd stay long enough to be polite, then disappear from everybody's life.

He continued scanning the room. Dump was putting it mildly. Clothes, clean and/or dirty, were piled willy-nilly. Books, boxes, black garbage bags of stuff, and loose miscellaneous stuff scattered around. He wondered how Susan liked picking up after him. She hadn't been peachy keen about Buckley's sloppiness.

How the hell had she lived *here*?

More pictures than he realized in the dark last night still hung on walls. Some were big enough to drive a car through. They were different and the same. In Buckley's view, the overriding theme was to make people guess what they were supposed to be, like quiz shows in frames. He supposed they'd eventually grow on you.

"Could you take the sentry duty for a minute?" Andrew asked.

"Some fugitives we are." Buckley eased out of the chair in slow motion. Any sudden movement after an undetermined amount of cheap wine, and his brain and skull would be clanging like a church bell.

Buckley folded back a section of an unfamiliar comic strip, wistful for L'il Abner and Buck Rogers.

"What do you see?"

"Buildings, cars, blue sky."

The sun made Buckley sneeze.

"No sudden moves or noises! We don't want an

overreaction that escalates!"

"Settle down, Andrew. You're giving me and all your neighbors the heebie-jeebies," Buckley said.

"Stay concealed and concentrate."

"Wow."

Andrew dropped what became pieces of broken china and scrambled to the window.

"A mourning dove on the sidewalk, see, next to the curb," Buckley said. They must be outnumbered by rock doves, common pigeons, by a hundred to one.

"Jesus, up at our level. Damn, there they go. Golden-crowned kinglets. You rarely see kinglets away from conifer forests and they're as nervous as hummingbirds. Two-ninety-five and two-ninety-six on my life list."

"Pardon me?"

"Birds. You're thinking commandos and black helicopters? You take birds as you find them."

"Misplaced priorities," Andrew muttered.

"There's no rush-hour traffic on the street," Buckley said. "It's eerie if you let your mind play tricks. They could have traffic cordoned off."

"It's Saturday. If a SWAT team is positioned, we would not see anything until they wanted us to."

"So how come we're giving ourselves eyestrain?"

"That's peculiar," Andrew said.

"What is?"

"The Corvette in front, it looks exactly like Stanley Buckley's."

"Oops."

"As you said, some fugitives we are. I was meaning to ask, and tell me if it is none of my concern, were you able to reconcile with your son?"

"We're making progress."

"I found Stanley to be distant, but perhaps I contributed to the alienation."

Perhaps with a capital P, Buckley didn't say.

The toaster popped. The room reeked of burnt toast and electrical fittings.

"Have breakfast before you go."

"Maybe more coffee."

A clicking noise at the door made both men flinch. The knob turned.

Andrew ran forward and threw up his hands.

"I surrender," he yelled. "I waive my right to an attorney."

Buckley pressed against a wall, away from the line of fire.

Bud Pogue walked in holding a steel pick. He was wearing yesterday's clothes, less the necktie.

Unlit cigarette tucked above his ear, he said, "Room for one more at this circle jerk? God, you guys look like death warmed over."

"I waive the right to remain silent." Andrew went on.

"Don't bother," Bud Pogue said. "Just shut the fuck up."

"You two are acquainted?" Andrew said. "I insist on seeing proper identification."

Buckley made quick introductions and said, "I'm impressed."

"Your friend know how to lock his door? I dusted off my B&E kit for no reason." Pogue sniffed. "What stinks?"

"Burned toast and unsafe wiring and turpentine," Buckley said.

"At least no decomposing flesh. I didn't know what to expect when you two jokers collided."

"Me neither," Buckley said.

"That you patched up differences without having to be patched up your ownselves, my hat's off to you," Pogue said.

"How'd you find me? Us?"

"Don't give me the credit. Mr. B's mom saw you poach Mr. B's car and the picture she'd thrown out. That plastic toy of his is loud enough to wake the dead. She put two and two together." Pogue yawned. "I been parked at the copper and brass works up the street half the fucking night, standing by in case I heard screaming and broken glass. I monitored your Boy Scout surveillance at the window and was fully prepared to boogie on up, a can of pepper spray in each hand. These your pictures too on the walls, Cardigan?"

"Paintings. Yes."

Pogue appraised the artwork, made no further comment, and opened the door. "It's safe."

Dotti Magnuson and Susan Buckley walked in.

"Good morning, Mr. Buckley," Dotti said.

Susan glared coldly at Andrew.

Buckley sucked in his gut and managed a hello. Dotti appeared crisp and desirable in gray pants suit and small briefcase.

In a sweat suit, Sooz was desirable too, *more* desirable as he compared them side by side. This in spite of her being grouchy and tired, probably sleepless in Seattle last night.

"I notified Ms. Magnuson's law firm and she was enthusiastic in regards to your situation," Pogue told Buckley.

"After last night's program, utterly fascinated," Dotti said.

Bud Pogue said, "You ladies will be pleased to learn that these yo-yos have spent the night here together, kissed and made up, and not a drop of blood was shed."

"You could of put that differently, Pogue," Buckley said.

"Where are my diaries?" Susan asked Andrew in a quiet cadence.

"You simply discarded *Trieste*?" Andrew retaliated weakly.

Susan's glare dropped the room temperature another ten degrees.

Andrew scrambled to heft a box onto the barrel beside the empty wine jug. The puny metal clasps were bent and broken. Andrew was no Mike the Locksmith.

"Is this all of them?" Susan asked sweetly, a steam boiler brimming with calmness. "Including the one responsible for your fifteen minutes of fame."

Andrew gulped and nodded.

"Including the framed photograph of Joe?"

"It's in there too."

"How'd you come up with the inspiration for this JFK beeswax?" Pogue asked him, then looked at Dotti. "I'd've gone for Goldwater had I been a registered voter. He'd of H-bombed Red China back into the Stone Age."

"Andrew, what in Heaven's name possessed you to go that far?" Susan added.

"I recommend you spill your guts while they're still attached to you," Buckley advised him.

Andrew did in detail, ending, "Isn't the absence of law enforcement intervention peculiar, especially the FBI or CIA?"

"Pretty easy for you to scoot out of Hollywood with your so-called evidence, don't you think?" Bud Pogue asked.

"Regardless, why aren't the authorities here confiscating them, hopefully violating my civil rights?" Andrew demanded.

"For Chrissake, quit your bellyaching," Buckley said. "No news is damn good news."

"I put out feelers," Pogue said, holding the unlit cigarette. "The only attention you'll have on your Kennedy hoopla is from wackos. Officialdom needs a helluva lot more than hot diary readings on some dipshit tabloid program to generate indictments, no offense, Ms. Buckley.

It's a royal pain in the bureaucratic pooper to reopen dead files. I also did a consult with the little honey in charge of computer security for Mr. B."

"The young woman in charge of computer security for Mr. B., Mr. Pogue," Dotti Magnuson corrected.

"That's what I said. She said there was some buzz, a tempest in a teapot that'll fizzle unless some hard evidence steps forward."

"But I saw with my own eyes, storm trooper types rushing in," Andrew cried.

Pogue said, "This sleazoid show's ratings have been sputtering. Your shtick didn't give them enough of a boost. What you saw with your own eyes, your Feebies, were probably actors. You were supposed to take the scene in, wet your britches, and head for the hills without your money, which you did exactly on cue."

Pogue looked at Buckley. "There's bigger fish for law enforcement to fry than Joseph Buckley."

"I am a harmless geezer," he said, nodding.

Pogue's eyes returned to Dotti's. "The Army desertion deal, on the other hand."

She unzipped her briefcase and withdrew a yellow legal pad. "When you visited me after your son's wedding, Mr. Buckley."

"Joe."

"God," Susan said.

"Joe," Dotti said, "Although you hadn't followed up with us, I did outline your predicament to my colleague, Ron. It was timely that Mr. Pogue touched base with me on your associated problems."

"I was gonna contact you shortly," Buckley said. "While we're at it, how 'bout we sue *Exclusive!!* for slander?"

"You may have a strong case."

"Yeah?"

"Eventually. Until your other issue is resolved, future litigation is not advisable."

"Yeah. I'm a man without a country."

"Ron networked with a major in the Army JAG he went to law school with."

"Networking is that buzzword they have for the swift service we're providing you," Pogue said, making a face.

Dotti stuck her tongue out at him. Buckley couldn't believe it! Dotti had fallen for him. Fallen hard and fast.

"Ron's JAG friend said your situation is unusual. Most Vietnam-era deserters fit two categories. New recruits who decided in Basic Training that the Army wasn't their cup of tea and those who moved to Canada upon receipt of orders to Vietnam. You were a career soldier and Vietnam veteran who reenlisted not long before."

"I took a Burst of Six," Buckley said. "Temporary insanity."

"There lies the rub. Ron's friend consulted a superior, who accessed your records. The rare Vietnam-era deserter who falls into official hands at this late date customarily is not court-martialed. He's given a less than honorable discharge and that's the end of it. But you have a complication."

"What else is new?"

"You did receive a reenlistment bonus, Joe?"

"Seventeen hundred bucks. A nice wad of dough in the sixties."

Dotti Magnuson read from her notes. "They'll make an issue of that bonus. They'll want it repaid."

"They're in an uproar over seventeen hundred bucks?" Buckley said. "How many cruise missiles would it buy?"

"Every penny in the Defense budget counts."

"One more penny in the billions they waste," Buckley said.

"Be that it may. It's official policy. Seventeen hundred

dollars less pro rata credit for the time you served prior to deserting. Terms are negotiable, but five-percent interest compounded quarterly is a likely repayment scenario."

"What's that add up to?"

"Nineteen thousand one hundred and twenty four dollars and forty-one cents."

Buckley groaned. "Nineteen grand and change."

"It has been thirty-five years," Dotti said.

"Time flies, podner," Bud Pogue said.

"What are the odds I'll receive *my* money from the TV swine?" Andrew asked Pogue and Dotti, his head swiveling jerkily.

"Did you sign a contract?" Dotti asked Andrew.

"They made the offer verbally and said they'd have their attorneys draw one up."

"When real-life swine can fly," Pogue said.

"I'm afraid he's right," Dotti Magnuson agreed.

Susan kissed Andrew's cheek, a definite finality in the peck. She picked up her box of diaries and went to the door. The party was over. Buckley shook the gloomy Andrew's hand and said thanks anyway for breakfast, maybe some other time.

A gallant Bud Pogue took Dotti Magnuson's hand as they descended the treacherous stairwell. Buckley, like a schoolboy, carried Susan's books, her hand extended to catch either him or the books if he lost his footing.

Pogue and Dotti peeled out in his company car.

Susan outstretched a palm. "Give me the keys, you big dope. I'll drive."

"I'm perfectly capable."

"You're still half drunk and if we're stopped for a burned-out taillight, then what?"

Buckley carefully rested the diaries on the Corvette hood and patted his pockets for the keys. Susan got in and started the car with the key he had left in the ignition.

*Gary Alexander*

# 18.

"**I**'ll catch a ride and pick up my rig later," Susan said, jamming the shifter into second, throwing Buckley's head back. "I never get to drive this hot rod. Your note was cute, as intimate as you're capable of being."

They passed her parked SUV in a blur. Buckley cinched his seat belt tighter. "Just trying to be informative."

"Did you ever write me love letters? I don't remember any."

"Nah. I whispered sweet obscenities in your ear. You're the literary Buckley."

"I could have died of humiliation in Stanley's theater. Andrew, that contemptible son of a bitch. He violated me, us, our relationship. It was as if he paraded us naked in front of a million voyeurs."

Buckley wished now he'd taken a poke at the beanpole. "Was Stan-Stanley a comfort to you? I saw him leave your wing."

"He was indeed. Thank you for asking. I couldn't help but notice the set of your jaw while you were committing grand theft auto. What on earth were you going to do with *Trieste*?"

"Nothing too awfully pleasant."

"As much as I despise that man, I have to grudgingly admit he is a talented painter. No contemporary abstract expressionist accomplishes what he does with negative space."

"Uh huh," was all Buckley could summon for "negative space".

"Beth and I had us a nice chat. You know, she's okay, basically a good egg," he added.

Susan laughed. "You and Beth? Will wonders never cease."

"Beth's looking out for her husband. If she sometimes acts snotty, that's how come. She's not gonna nominate me as father of the year and she's worried my woes will rub off on him. She's also of a mind that the boy's interest in his Uncle Stan borders on the weird. I have to agree with her on all charges. Another thing, Beth yakked in Stan-Stanley's ear just prior to him leaving his theater and visiting you. It was her idea if I'm not mistaken."

"I'll try harder with Beth, Joe."

"While I doubt you'd do it if you were in Beth's shoes, her nudging you out the door so her own mother can have your place, I suppose, is natural."

"Please, enough already. You and your nocturnal stunt, you had me worried sick."

"Sorry. I was sneaking out to the best of my ability, not to cause you to lose a night's sleep."

"You were unsuccessful. I panicked and called Bud, bless his heart. He was in Portland and came on up immediately."

Portland. The mention brought Buckley's immature yearning for Dotti tumbling to the pit of his stomach. If anything made a woman unbearably attractive, it was being aced out for her affections. That Dotti ran a distant second to Sooz in his hit parade was irrelevant.

"Yeah. What's going on there?"

"After Bud phoned your lawyer, he went down there to work on your case. They came here together when I called him. Evidently Cupid's arrows are flying."

"Evidently."

"She seems to be a positive influence. Poor lovesick Bud, he won't light a cigarette in her presence."

"A nicotine fit is no fun at all," Buckley said. "It's a helluva sacrifice."

"Tell me about it. You and Andrew absolutely shocked me. There were no signs of violence and *Trieste* was intact."

"We kind of bonded, believe it or not."

"Did you talk about me?"

"Not much. I chopped him off when he pissed and moaned about your diaries. I also swore on a stack of Bibles that nothing happened between us after the wedding."

"Did he swallow your malarkey?"

"Nope."

"Joseph Buckley, you can be a gem, you know. I'm adding Andrew to my long list of learning experiences. If I hadn't behaved like an old slut at Cannon Beach, I might never have known that he was an even more flawed human being than *moi*."

"You and him shacked up in that crackerbox? I couldn't stand that turpentine smell myself."

"Did I mention that I'm self-destructive too? We share *folie à deux*. Haven't you figured that out by now?"

"Folly a doo-doo to you too, you little college girl. I haven't figured out how to spell half the words you use so I could look them up in the dictionary, providing I wanted to. Living there in Andrew's dump, that's above and beyond."

"He was partially truthful that I lived there. I was a regular overnight visitor. That I kept a toothbrush and a few things on hangers there pleased him and assuaged his insecurities. I was still waiting tables when we met and had my own apartment. I'd sold my house and socked the money away for retirement."

"Planning ahead's a wise approach," Buckley said. "Better late than never is my motto."

"I'll probably look nostalgically on this as my Bohemian Period, the romance of artistic promise and squalor. We ladies have midlife crises too. Andrew was highly respected at school and he was mine, all mine. In retrospect, he was after my money before I had real money"

"Real money, I hear, is putting it mildly."

"Bud apologized to me for letting the cat out of the bag that I own twenty percent of sjbWare. He said you nearly fell off your barstool. He thought you knew I was loaded."

"I didn't think you were a bag lady. But holy cow. I'm happy for you, Sooz, I truly am."

"Joe, your problems, frankly, are trivial. A little money can make them go away. Poof."

"No."

"Joe, nineteen thousand dollars is pin money to me."

"Nope."

"Making you a long-term, low-interest loan would be enjoyable, Joe."

"I've never taken advantage of a gal. For money."

"God, how many more times do I have to listen to that one?"

"Besides, Uncle Sam gouging me, it's the principle of the thing. Piss on them. They can go straight to hell. All that interest, they're like the goddamn Mafia."

"You're all screwed up, Joe Buckley."

"When did I ever claim I wasn't?"

She downshifted the Corvette, goosed it, and went under a yellow light. "Your misguided chivalry rears up at the oddest moments. Unfortunately, it charmed me off my feet and still does."

"I'll be fine, Sooz. Thanks for the offer."

"Well, you do have your restaurant in Belize. I apologize for doubting your solvency."

Buckley cleared his throat. "Well, I had one of those

hostile takeovers at Molly's you see on CNN."

"Meaning?"

"A couple of Brits pulled the rug out from under me. Long story. Anyway, I'm anxious to go home, but I'm in no gigantic hurry on account of business reasons."

"I'm so sorry, Joe."

"No sweat. As far as self-employment goes, I'm better suited for tour guiding in the great out of doors. So that's what I'll do down there. My life list is nearly three hundred."

Susan shook her head. "The bird man of Belize. You are a piece of work. How do you plan to get home?"

"Fly."

"You know what I mean, wisenheimer."

"I'll speak to my travel agent in Belize City, see what he can arrange."

"Who is?"

"Just a guy who provides necessary documents. For a price."

"Some criminal lowlife forger?"

"Name-calling is beneath you, Sooz."

"Let's see what you have?"

Buckley dug the Harold Roy Qwerty passport out of his pocket and gave it to her. "The guy I'm pretending to be is Albanian."

Susan looked at it and began laughing. And laughing. Laughing as hard as Dotti Magnuson had when they first met. Also laughing until she cried.

"What's the big joke, Sooz?"

"Q-w-e-r-t-y is the joke and the joke's on you."

"He's not Albanian?"

"Joe, next time you're near a typewriter or a computer keyboard, check out the first six letters in the upper left."

"Qwerty is a fake name on a forged passport?"

"Phony as a three-dollar bill, Joe."

"A forged passport. A phony," he said, shaking his head.

"Okay, Buckley, do this for me and for yourself. Since you're here, since you're in the neighborhood, as they say, stick around an extra day or two."

"I feel like a ping pong ball."

"Do they celebrate Father's Day in Belize?"

"No."

"Father's Day is tomorrow."

"It is?"

"Will you?"

"It'd be awkward."

"It doesn't have to be if everybody keeps everything in perspective. Stanley's at work as usual. I'll ask him later. He and Beth are having a little barbecue. Charles will be there also."

"Maybe."

"We'll studiously avoid the F-word and the S-word."

"I promise I won't cuss."

"Father. Son. It shouldn't be too uncomfortable. I seriously doubt if Beth is going out of her way for her father and Puberty Girl. They're having sjbWare friends too. The barbecue really is generic."

"Drop me at a motel. I'll think about it."

"Not on your life. You're being shanghaied for your own good."

Buckley patted her thigh. "I accept your kind invitation."

She looked at him. "Living restrictions are unchanged."

"Sure. Pull over here for a minute."

The stopped at a convenience store. Buckley bought both Seattle dailies and a *USA Today*. He spread them out on the Corvette trunk. Susan helped scan the papers, chasing the pages that blew away.

Searching reluctantly for himself, Buckley came to a business section and the headline: LOCAL FIRM DEFIES TECH DOWNTOWN TREND.

"Lookie!" Buckley said, jabbing his son's photograph. "Wow!"

Susan squeezed his arm. "I'm happy you're excited. I was too the first twenty or fifty times I saw him in print or on TV."

"On TV too?"

"Stanley and sjbWare are big news locally. The company is making an impact on area high-tech employment. What have you found on the treasonous Private First Class Buckley?"

"Zip," Buckley said. "Zilch. Not a single, solitary word."

"Bud said there was no credibility to that ridiculous presentation and he was right. I am a little surprised, though."

"Me too. Looks like Andrew's career has stalled out where it is and I'd best skedaddle before Uncle comes after his nineteen grand."

"Not until after tomorrow, Joe."

"No problem."

"Your attorney, Ms. Magnuson, is delightful and she's bright. She will do a terrific job on your behalf."

"That was my evaluation."

"Her and Bud, that's an odd couple. She's very 'with it' and he's on every feminist police enemies list."

"Definitely an odd couple," Buckley agreed.

"Dotti Magnuson is also, relatively speaking, Buckley, jailbait for either one of you two horny old characters."

Looking at the road again, Susan pulled out and deposited low-gear rubber.

"You should talk about robbing the cradle."

She smiled. "Touché."

"Something's funny."

"What?"

"You haven't blown your stack once at me since we've been in the car."

"My, that is unusual."

"And that telepathy stuff we always had going, not once did I read your mind."

"Nor I yours. You realize what that means, Joe. We're starting again from scratch, you and I."

She paused and added, "That's terrifying."

"You got that right," Buckley said.

# 19.

"Hey, Philip."

After several seconds of static: "Who is this speaking?"

"Buckley. Joe Buckley."

"Who?"

"The businessman from San Ignacio."

"San Ignacio? You there now?"

"I wish."

"And you are who, sir?"

"Think Harold Roy Qwerty of Colorado. I went up to the States for my son's wedding."

"Yeah. How'd that go?"

"The wedding went fine."

"Where you at?"

A steel band in the background made Buckley agonizingly homesick, parched for a cold Belikin. "Still up in the States. I have a problem."

"Don't we all, man. How's the weather?"

"I'm freezing my ass and my luggage was stolen."

"That is a low blow. You can't even bundle up."

"Everything important was in it, if you catch my drift."

"Everything?"

"Including Joe Buckley. Harold Roy Qwerty needs a Joe Buckley replacement for Joe Buckley's return trip. Mr. Qwerty is a phony name."

"What're you saying, man?"

"You borrowed a fake passport is what I'm saying."

"The guy swindled and cheated me?"

"Afraid so."

"You can't trust anybody these days."

"Irregardless, I need a passport."

"How can I replace one for you if you ain't here?"

"Make it up in my name and mail it up here pronto."

"Forgery? You asking me to forge? I got my standards."

"You're not forging, Philip. You're kind of duplicating. You're doing a me of me for me. It's almost legal."

"Says you."

"C'mon, do up a set and mail it, for Chrissake. Mail it fast."

"Mail to you up there in the States?"

"Please."

"This will be expensive."

"Already was and that was for a counterfeit. I oughta get a discount on account of that. Have anything handy?"

"Mm, I'm looking. Here is a gent, a little fuller in the face, but in your general age group. The photo could pass."

"Great. Do your magic. Can you ship it to me on some overnight package carrier? I'll pay you when I see you in Belize City."

"I have an idea. You pay me and then I mail to you."

"How?"

"I got an account for special customer service needs such as yours. It's a brand-new state-of-the-art-leading-edge-kind-of-thing this smart computer guy I met taught me when I got him out of a little jam involving offshore funds and an underage gal who really did look older.

"How it works is, I give you numbers and a computer address. You open an account and deposit cash. You type in the address and numbers on a computer, and transfer money from your account to mine. I see the transaction on my computer, the item is as good as in the air to you. Easy."

"So you won't trust me for the money?"

"Man, what it comes down to, one of us got to trust the other. I'd rather it be me to carry the burden of your trust. There are extra expenses too."

"I don't object to paying the shipping and handling."

"The bigger expense is to my good name and my freedom if the clerk I hand your merchandise to don't like my looks and has suspicions regarding the contents. Then I got to pay him to go temporary blind."

"I don't know. You're gonna be too rich for my thin blood, Philip. Doesn't me being your oldest, steadiest customer mean anything?"

"My phone is breaking up, man. We're losing reception."

"Okay, okay, deal, but you've probably never thought of using a phony name, huh?"

"Belize City is a tiny small town."

Buckley threw in the towel. He gave Philip the vitals on himself and wrote down a string of numbers and letters. The bank account code, some www-dot-gobbledygook, and Just Philip's price.

"How about an arm and leg too?" he said.

"You stranded yourself up there in the Arctic climates, man. Your opportunity to come on home is a bargain at any price. Go do this on a computer."

"Sure. I'll pull a computer out of a hat."

"You can go into these shops they have and rent the use of one. One of those Internet cafés. The process is child's play."

Not amused, Joe Buckley laughed.

# 20.

**B**uckley dangled his bare feet off the dock, wiggling his toes in the drink, binoculars poised. Gentle swells lapped against his son's boat, making slurping noises. In that scattered flotilla out on the lake, almost no craft was longer or taller or wider or shinier.

The occasional cloud puff steered clear of the sun. It was a warm day, not hot, a fine day for birding. Buffleheads and American coots floated and fished, a hundred yards out. Two entire different species of waterfowl, each predominately black and white, coexisted without mingling. The buffleheads were divers, doing somersaults and vanishing. Buckley was wondering how they could hold their breath so long when Stanley Buckley joined him, just home from work.

"I bet you thought you'd seen the last of me."

"How could I? You didn't say good-bye."

Stanley remained standing. He was holding a plump manila folder. Looking into the sun, Buckley couldn't see his face well enough to read it, and his tone was neutral, either hurt or pissed or matter-of-fact, take your choice. The fat lip was nearly a memory, no larger than a boil.

A Caspian tern did a fly-over. Number 297.

Buckley sneezed. "Sorry 'bout the car heist. I thought it best to get out of your hair before the heat was cranked up even hotter."

"Not a problem. According to Bud, any dogged official pursuit regarding any of your issues is highly unlikely."

"So far, so good. I'm pleased for everybody concerned."

"Mom told me about you and Andrew. There has not been a dull moment hereabouts lately."

"I seem to have that effect, as your mother will verify." Buckley pointed down the shoreline. "Lookie. The dead snag at the peak of the tallest tree. A bald eagle. I saw him the other day."

"Cool."

If the younger Buckley had looked, it was an eyeblink glance. He opened the folder. "Your departure delay is opportune. This was delivered today as I was leaving the office."

He pulled out a binder and handed it to Buckley. The top sheet carried the letterhead of a private detective agency.

"Subject is Taylor Smyth. Who's Taylor Smyth?"

"My paternal grandfather."

Buckley wobbled to his feet, numbed by cool water and shock. "My old man? Really?"

"Unquestionably. My DNA and Taylor Smyth's DNA match."

"He's alive?"

"Remarkably, yes. He is. Taylor Smyth is an eighty-six year old retired logger, a resident of a Eugene, Oregon nursing home."

"This must've been some project, hunting him down."

"It was," Stan said, pinching fingers around the half-inch-thick binder. "The search process was laborious and is documented, line by line. The detectives I hired requested DNA tests from the candidates still living."

"They all agreed to?"

"Yes. We approached them without specifics, stating that they may have an adult offspring they're unaware of. The majority complied out of curiosity, including Mr. Smyth. The others did when we offered payment."

"How many were curious for a price?"

"Fourteen."

"Your gramma was no saint," Buckley said.

"That was my initial impression. Perhaps we shouldn't be too harsh. She and Mr. Smyth had a long relationship."

"How come I don't remember him?"

"The relationship was sporadic and volatile. Taylor Smyth was married. To the same woman for sixty-one years, as a matter of fact. His wife died four years ago."

"They were playing it cool, huh?" Buckley said.

"They were. Mr. Smyth remembered your mother with affection."

"A little support would've been nice too."

"We believe he did contribute a few dollars now and again. He couldn't afford much. He had seven children of his own."

Buckley whistled.

"Most are currently living in western Oregon."

"Amazing. I got me a bunch of step-families."

"Would you like to visit Taylor Smyth?"

"I don't know. My head's spinning."

"Mine too. I might run down next week and meet him."

"I'll be gone. I'll have to catch him next trip."

"He's not in the best of health."

"No offense, but my feelings and misgivings about him are probably more complex than yours."

"None taken," Stanley said. "Though I may be idealizing him, I had the sense he and my grandmother looked after each other to the utmost of their limited abilities. I'm traveling to Eugene anyhow to introduce myself and try to clear up something the investigators couldn't. Mr. Smyth's memory is fuzzy. He doesn't recall the chronology when he was in my grandmother's life, nor was he precise on Uncle Stan."

"Whether he fathered him?"

"Yes."

"My guess is no. I was a piece of work, yeah. In comparison, that gunslinger was completely off the deep end. We weren't close, ever, and we didn't look alike. We were rarely mistaken as brothers."

"Uncle Stan's buried in a pauper's grave in Salem. We could easily settle the issue with a DNA test."

"Grave robbing?"

"Legal exhumation. I presume that it's no more complicated than you as closest surviving relative signing a paper to initiate the process. I'll have our house counsel look into it. If you'd be willing."

Laying out *if you'd be willing* not exactly as a question, laying it out as casually as a dinner check to be signed. This was getting creepy, the subject itself, and more so, the non-expression on his boy's face.

On the other hand, what the hell's the difference? Disrespecting the dead wasn't a consideration. Buckley and his brother had enjoyed no mutual respect in life. If their places were reversed, Big Stan would sign on the dotted line in an instant if the price was right.

"No sweat. Send me the papers."

"Thank you. I will. While the investigators were in Oregon, I asked them to clarify the circumstances of Uncle Stan's final showdown with the police. He did have a revolver, a blue-steel Colt Cobra thirty-eight caliber six-shot double action with a three-inch barrel. He got off one shot that ricocheted off a light standard. Uncle Stan took eighteen police bullets in return. Per the autopsy, any of seven could have been the fatal round. Luckily nobody else was hurt."

Jesus, talking like it was OK Corral.

"Yeah, luckily."

"Mom mentioned tomorrow to you?"

"She did."

"I hope you can make it."

"Hey, sure, thanks. I oughta be outta here for good on Monday."

"You can take the Corvette wherever you have to go to catch your flight. I'll send someone for it. If you'd like to stay longer and feel legal ramifications continue to hang over your head, use the Cannon Beach place as a hideout."

Hideout. "That's mighty generous."

"All you have to do is ask."

His face flushing, Buckley studied his fingernails. "Ever catch *Leave It to Beaver* on the tube?"

"A cable channel reran episodes several years ago. Was family life really that blissful?"

"Not for me it wasn't. It kind of is now, you and me here, except we seem to have the Ward and Beaver roles backasswards."

Stan laughed. "There's no emotional obligation tomorrow, okay?"

"Okay."

They shook on it.

"Chuck will be there too."

"Chuck?"

"Formerly known as Charles, Beth's father."

"Yeah, that's right. And the little woman?"

"Heather. They're inseparable."

"That'll be worth the price of admission alone."

Father and son shared a laugh, then turned to heavy footfalls on the dock.

Bud Pogue lumbered toward them. He retrieved a half-smoked cigarette tucked above his ear and lit up in an impatient motion, life a 1950s greaser late for class, cadging a puff behind the gym.

Stanley Buckley reclaimed the folder. "Please don't bring this up. Although he already has plenty on his plate, Bud would be hurt that I'd outsourced the investigation assignment without inviting him into the loop."

"Mum's the word."

Pogue drew a long drag to the floor of his chest, then field-stripped the butt into the water before he reached the Buckleys.

"Say what you want of unfiltered cancer sticks," he said, smoke drifting from his nostrils. "They're superior to filters in a major respect. Remember police call in the Army, Buckley?"

"Oh yeah."

"After morning formation, Mr. B," he said to his boss. "They'd march the troops from the barracks to the company street, the parade grounds, or some vacant lot, and spread you out in a line. You'd stoop and walk slow to the other end, policing up what there was to police up."

"Thus the expression," Stan said.

"There you are. Eighty percent of what you policed up was cigarette filters, especially after it'd rained. The rest of the cigarette was gone, biodegraded, healthy for the environment. From then on, to me, any GI who smoked filter tips was an inconsiderate pussy."

Pogue cocked his head. Dotti Magnuson and Susan were chatting outside the coach house, Beth and Irene too, off to a side. "Dotti, she's a sweet, attractive lady for a health nut. I offered to roll down all windows and stick out my head to exhale. She said no way José, unless you stop and let me out."

"Bud," Stan said. "Are you doing anything tomorrow?"

"What's tomorrow? Sunday. Depends on what develops."

Buckley looked at him, then Dotti, who waved. His butterflies restless, Buckley waved back.

"We're having an informal barbecue," Stan said. "Two o'clock. Swing by if you're available. Feel free to bring a guest."

"In that case, sir, I am available. I accept your kind invite."

Bud took a business envelope out of a pocket and gave it to Buckley. "This here is a representation agreement Attorney Magnuson brought up from Portland. Because of the flap at that fag hippie artist colony Cardigan lives at, she didn't think it right to whip it on you there.

"She had some T's to dot and I's to cross also, so we went to my office where while she worked I watched Mr. B's young pups, on their breaks, play foosball, wired on Mountain Dew. If it's A-OK, toss it and your retainer in the mail, and they'll proceed."

"I'll check it over," Buckley said. "Shouldn't be a problem."

Bud Pogue met Dotti Magnuson, who called back to Buckley. "Joe, if you have any questions, my cell phone number is in the cover letter."

Buckley managed a smile and a thank you. Pogue escorted Dotti to his company car, arm around her, not quite touching.

Conquest, before or after? Outright ownership? Dotti didn't seem the ownership type, unless she was doing the owner-shipping.

As Beth and her mother were entering the house, Buckley caught Irene's eye and fixed upon her his dirtiest, let's-get-us-a- motel-room, barroom leer.

She replied with a puzzled glare and backpedaled inside.

"Playing the field, Buckley?" Susan asked, approaching.

"Just testing the shark-infested waters. A fella has to wear blinders around you."

"Stanley mentioned tomorrow?"

"I'll be happy to attend. Honored."

"Have you studied your lawyer's paperwork?"

"Not yet and it might not be feasible. I called my travel agent," he said, relating his conversation with Just Philip and how he swindled him on the Qwerty passport whether he knew he was flimflamming him or not.

Susan sighed, speechless.

"I have the dough, but this computer thing, it's all Greek."

"Your fifteen minutes of fame have expired and you're riding off into the sunset."

"You got it."

"Come upstairs. We'll take care of your quote-unquote travel agent. I can do the transfer from my account."

"On your computer?"

"It won't bite. Besides, I'll bribe you with a cold beer."

Susan's wing was a mix of old and new, mostly the latter, new and pricey, plenty of chrome and glass and leather. A swayback, threadbare orange couch in a den dominated by a giant TV was faintly familiar.

"It isn't."

"It is. Ours. We had it in Tacoma, when we lived in the second floor slum on Pacific Highway."

Buckley uncapped beers, gave Susan hers, took a long swig, and said, "The dump that had critter noise inside the walls at night, mice eating the insulation."

"We didn't have any insulation. They were eating the wiring. Cold drafts came straight through the walls like needles."

"What do you want for seventy bucks a month including garbage and water?"

Buckley stared at the couch, remembering now activities on it other than television watching. He told her about the Taylor Smyth revelation.

"Wow," Susan said. "Good for Stanley. He's extremely tenacious, you know. How do you feel, Joe?"

Buckley shrugged. "I'm still dazed."

"I don't blame you. Discovering at age sixty that you're not an orphan after all must be traumatic."

"The guano about brother Stan bothers me worse. Him shooting it out with the cops was a turn-on to Stan-ley. I tell you, Sooz, I'm a bad influence on my boy."

"Nobody would disagree. You could visit this Taylor Smyth with Stanley. You might regret it if you don't."

"It'd be awkward. What if his seven kids and their kids and their kids' kids popped in? Fifty's a crowd if you're the odd man out."

Buckley stopped, white-knuckled his beer, and said, "Sooz, it's all of a sudden hit me. Boom, bam, pow! You know, those old sci-fi movies where you go back in a time machine and change your life, that's what I'd be doing cuz Taylor Smyth was never in my life and I never had a father and I'd be seeing how it might've been and everything would look different from here on forward, cuz of how it could've been. I told you in the old days what it was like growing up in a hick town without a daddy's last name, whether he was in the picture or not.

"I was Joe Buckley, and Stan and me were Madeline Buckley's boys and everybody knew she'd never married, not that I'm blaming Smyth for us turning out as fuck-ups, but when you're a kid in school and you get called a whore's bastard, you punch him in the fucking mouth. At least that's how I handled the situation.

"My mom, she was a drunk and a tramp and we never had anything on account of her working odd jobs, cleaning houses and doing laundry and whatever she could do, when she was fit to work, but she was our mom and she did the best she could, no thanks to Smyth or anyone else.

"I'm not Joe Smyth, I'm Joe Buckley. Taylor Smyth, if he even remembers back that long ago, he'd be sticking me in that time machine and when we were done I'd be stepping out in the here and now and not a damn thing would of changed."

Buckley covered his eyes and faced the wall. Reminded of standing in the corner when he misbehaved in class, the tear flow increased.

Susan hugged the trembling Buckley.

"Gimme a second, okay?"

When he'd wiped his cheeks on his arms and was ready, she led him into the next room, which was much smaller, the principal item of décor being a fully outfitted computer desk, a screen and keyboard and other plastic gizmos full of buttons.

He gestured to the chair. "Have at it."

"No, Joe. Sit down. You're going to do it. Thanks to our son, one household in a thousand has a system this advanced. We're directly wired to sjbWare servers."

"I know about servers, but c'mon, Sooz."

"Sit."

Buckley sat.

"Qwerty. I see it."

"Good boy."

"That is a lot of money for forged ID."

"Revised ID. In my own name. There's a big difference."

"Please don't spill your beer on the keyboard. The button on the box standing on end on your right the size of your thumb, push it."

Buckley pushed. Beep, buzz, whir, chirp, chirp, blinking lights. After the screen finally lit up, the thing calmed down. The background was a picture of sjbWare Headquarters. Susan called it a desktop and a screensaver. She put his hand on the gadget she called a mouse (he already knew what a mouse was) and steered it to one of a couple dozen tiny pictures superimposed over sjbWare.

She pushed his index finger down twice.

"Congratulations, Joe. You double-clicked on and accessed my Internet service provider."

"Swell. We double-pushed."

"Clicked."

"Whatever."

A busy screen of writing and pictures covered up the sjbWare complex. Before they went further, Susan took the mouse from him, pulled up a laundry list of programs, and proudly pointed out sjbBoost.

She said they were running beta test Version 4.1, which wouldn't be rolled out until late fall.

Buckley said whoopee.

Susan had him type some www-dot-gibberish into a box. He eventually accomplished the task, pounding away with two stiff index fingers. She took him step by step through more screens. Bank logos and pages appeared. More damn blanks to plug numbers galore into.

Buckley said, "When are we gonna be done?"

"Hit the 'Enter' key and you are."

"No kidding?"

"Was that so hard?"

Buckley swiveled around. "You looking over my shoulder, a cinch. It's all Greek to me."

"What do you think you're doing, Mr. Roaming' Hands?"

"Starting again from scratch."

"Wait a sec. Aren't we supposed to be dating first?"

"We already are. By my reckoning, not counting the beach, we've had four."

"That's two more before the first time we hopped in the sack."

"We're getting behind," Buckley said, pulling her onto his lap.

"Want to see the rest of my digs?"

"You betcha."

Next stop, a bedroom. The bed looked as big to Buckley as San Ignacio's town soccer pitch, two pillows and a fluffy pink silky spread on top.

"The blue toothbrush in the adjoining bath is new. It can be yours."

That was the end of the grand tour.

After Susan had her way with him, she said, "Now isn't this better than a quick roll with a forty-something teeny bopping bubble-gummer lawyer or Irene Cold Pants?"

"Yeah," Buckley said, nuzzling her, holding on for all he was worth. "Oh yeah."

# 21.

A scorcher, a record-breaker.

That's what TV weather folk were forecasting, the hottest June 18 ever recorded in the Seattle area. It was Father's Day morning and already 70-degrees. Ninety-one was predicted for the high. The previous mark of 88° didn't have a prayer.

Ninety-plus degrees Fahrenheit, hardly any humidity, fifty or sixty percent tops. An absolutely perfect day. Joe Buckley was in hog heaven.

He was sitting up in bed, channel surfing, energized after a night of blissful exhaustion. He had an idea, an impulse, and nudged Susan semi-awake.

"Sooz, hey, I'm gonna volunteer to do the food today."

"Huh?"

"The cooking, the food for the party."

"Uh."

"After all, I am a culinary professional."

"Um."

"Wait. Unless they're having it catered. Yeah, forget it. They would be."

"Uh uh."

Buckley spoke to a pillowed mop of silver hair. "Uh uh? Uh uh? They aren't?"

"Uh uh. Wanna do selves. Leave me alone."

Buckley dressed quickly and headed to the palace to run his offer by Beth Buckley, the lady of the mansion. The side door was ajar. Buckley went inside and immediately swooned at the sight of the industrial kitchen, all stainless steel and marble islands and hanging copperware, everything gleaming and immaculate. Most restaurant kitchens were broiling medieval galleys, space so tight that comings and goings had to be choreographed to minimize accidents. Grease spilled from a skillet meant a trip to the emergency room.

Beth Buckley was holding a lined pad, already wilting, fanning herself with a hot pad.

"Good morning," she said. "This is the only time we've had to put the air conditioning to the test and it turns out to be broken. Good luck getting someone out on the hottest Sunday of the year."

Buckley felt fine, damn near perky. He formally volunteered his services.

"That's sweet. But since our gathering is small, fifteen to eighteen people, I'd had planned on tackling the job myself, to try out my new kitchen, a burst of domesticity before going back to work."

"Hey, I can be your scullery maid or whatnot."

Beth smiled. "I may take you up on that. Who could have dreamed of this heat? And frankly, while I have a stuffed larder, I have no menu firmly in motion."

"I am a master improviser," Buckley said. "Let's see what we got."

Beth opened the fridge and said, "Spare ribs."

Which was as far as she got. Clinging to the handle, leaning her face against the refrigerator door, her knees buckled. Joe charged around an island. Arm circling her waist, hand gripping the forearm that rested limply on his shoulder, he walked her to the breakfast nook and lowered her into a chair.

"I'll call someone," he said. "Stan-ley."

"He's at work."

"An ambulance, Susan, your mother?"

"No, I'm all right. Honestly. A glass of water would hit the spot."

Buckley scrambled to the sink and threw open a cabinet. The first tumbler would have broken on the floor if it hadn't been plastic. He filled the second. She thanked him and asked him to sit too and please relax.

She took a drink. "It's all right, really. I feel good now. They say a little dizziness is normal if you overdo it. This heat. And I'm stressed out about the party."

"Who says it's normal?"

"My doctor when I saw her late last week."

It?

"Not serious, I hope," Buckley said.

Beth smiled like he'd never seen her smile. He didn't recognize her. "Oh, it's as serious as it can be."

"It is?"

Jesus H. Christ, if she had some dread disease, how come she's grinning like the Cheshire cat, like she's lost her marbles?

"Oh," he said, getting it. "Holy cow!"

Beth held a fingertip to her lips.

"Oh," Buckley repeated.

"I got the results of the test yesterday. Nobody knows, not even Stanley or Mother. I haven't decided yet how to break the news."

"Wow. Congratulations. You're not still going to work tomorrow, are you?"

"I am. I'm not hoeing potatoes, you know."

She squeezed his hand. "This is our secret. Isn't it?"

"On one condition. You take me up on my offer."

She shook the hand she squeezed.

"Deal. Meanwhile, I'll organize the place settings."

"While taking it easy," Buckley added. "Pacing yourself."

"Yes sir."

Further energized by being needed, being a confidant, Joe Buckley went wild, a veritable whirling dervish. He started boiling potatoes and eggs for salad, then mixed a barbecue sauce recipe he'd tinkered with for years, and set the baby back ribs to marinating. He deboned chicken thighs and breasts, and rubbed on a garlic-rosemary-oil mixture.

In a bowl the size of a radar dome, he whipped up a green salad composed of four different lettuces, arugula, julienned carrots, cherry tomatoes, shredded purple cabbage for accent, and cruets of balsamic vinaigrette and blue cheese dressing for application at the table.

Buckley had purpose. He was pulling his own strings.

There was a half bag of spuds left over. He sliced them paper-thin in a food processor powerful enough to winch an 18-wheeler out of a gully, then deep-fried chips in a fortune's worth of peanut oil. As soon as they cooled, he ate two handfuls for breakfast, washed them down with a cold beer, and went outside to organize his cooking stations.

Built into the patio was a partitioned barbecue-smoker combo that'd accommodate a half steer. Neither had been used, not once. The grill was as shiny as a new coin. Buckley got the smoker going and put in the ribs. They'd be at their best done low and slow. He could grill his chicken on either charcoal or gas.

Buckley preferred the former. He went into the garage and saw the Schwinn leaning on a wall, ready to go. He located a bag of mesquite briquettes, dumped them in the pit, and lit his fire.

Susan appeared, dabbed sauce from a side of Buckley's rib bowl, licked her finger, and said, "This is incredible, the best I've ever tasted."

"A secret recipe passed on to me by Belize's finest chef."

"Give it to me."

"On her death bed. I'm sworn to secrecy."

"Buckley."

"Nope. A secret's a secret."

"And last night will be a memory."

"A cinch to make," Buckley blurted. "Four parts of an ordinary supermarket bottled sauce, the kind they don't get cute adding extra flavors to. One part honey or agave nectar to cut the vinegar. And a splash of soy sauce."

"Good boy. Beth was okay about you running this show?"

*My son knocked up his girlfriend.*

"Peachy keen. She has to prepare to go back to the office tomorrow."

"We're kind of peachy keen too. Beth and I just made a truce. She acts different. Perhaps it's the heat. I'm serving as co-hostess. Stanley went in to the office."

"On a Sunday," Buckley said, shaking his head. "Won't that computer stuff keep for one day a week?"

"He usually goes in for only half a day. Less than a third of sjbWare's twelve hundred employees regularly work on Sunday, so he can catch up on his backlog with fewer interruptions."

"Is it worth it?" Buckley wondered out loud.

Susan flapped her blouse to cool herself.

"Feast your eyes around you, Buckley. You be the judge. Everybody has to decide."

****

Stan-ley arrived home carrying a briefcase as Buckley was checking his ribs.

"Beth called and said you're cooking."

"Yep. Yes I am."

"We appreciate this, but you're a guest. You shouldn't overdo it in this heat."

Shouldn't overdo it at your age, Buckley knew he was saying. He closed the smoker lid, waved at the fumes stinging his eyes, and saw that the boy was perspiring.

"The weather's ideal for my thinned-out, Belizean blood. I know fifty executive chefs who would give their left nut to work in a kitchen and a barby like yours. Believe me, I'm having a blast."

Shades of Vietnam, Buckley heard chopper blades, then saw a helicopter appear just above the trees. It hovered, sashayed its tail, and gently settled onto the coach house roof. A heliport too, and why the hell not?

It was a Bell, the civilian version of the Vietnam Huey, sjbWare logos painted on the sides. A guy in aviator coveralls and sunglasses hustled down back stairs Buckley didn't know existed, gave Stan an insulated sack, and was gone, him and his copter, just like that.

"In case you become dehydrated." He took out a six-pack of Belikin, brown bottles, the unmistakable Mayan temple printed on them, and presented it to Buckley. "We have branch offices. My Southwestern Zone manager in L.A. and I were on the phone. We gravitated to the subject of beer. I asked if he'd heard of your Belikin. He said he'd seen it on shelves. I asked for a favor. He came through. Enjoy."

The boy was blushing, red as a lobster.

Buckley said, "If you'll have one too."

Before Stan could protest, Buckley uncapped a pair and proposed a toast. "To an offspring better than I deserve."

Stan clinked his father's bottle and glanced at his watch. "To a new beginning. I have to change. Guests are coming."

"Later," Buckley said, sure that sjbWare troops had jumped through their behinds to expedite the six-pack for the boss man, maybe even flying it up on a private jet.

A Father's Day gift without Susan's F-word thrown in. A dandy!

This had been their defining moment, when they

became father and son again. Two guys and a six-pack.

If Susan was eavesdropping and wrote it up in her diary, she'd fiction it up with hugs and sobs and forgiveness, that ladies' afternoon talk show guano. Relatively speaking, guy behavior as opposed to gal, she'd be fairly accurate in regard to the end result.

Stan hurried inside, Belikin to his lips. If the boy's eyes had gotten wet, nobody was gonna see. If Buckley's did, a distinct possibility, he'd flip up the smoker lid and blame it on the smoke, the TLC he was giving the baby backs. He'd had the waterworks on more this past week than he had the last forty years.

\*\*\*\*

Party time. The guests exceeded thirty and counting.

Not a problem for Joe Buckley. In this business you guesstimated your food prep on the high side, expensive leftovers such as pork and chicken turning up tomorrow in casserole-type lunch specials partnered to rice and beans. That and/or the soup of the day.

Stan and Beth, matched as if twins in khaki and blue, gamely rolled shiny new wheelbarrows out of the garage. They were mounded with chopped ice, bottles of beer and soda and wine stuck in them like pinfeathers. Buckley exhaled in relief when she didn't have a fainting episode.

*My boy knocked up his girlfriend.*

The gang applauded. They were mostly carbon copies of Stan and Beth, plenty of eyeglasses and technical yakkety-yak, Em-dac and the rest.

As they sweltered under umbrellas, scarfing down his chips and taking in vital bodily fluids, Buckley tinkered again with his ribs and began grilling chicken.

Partygoers kept a cautious distance as he worked, though they sneaked peeks at the bare arm sporting the headless eagle. When he caught them looking, he couldn't resist flexing his biceps as he handled the tongs. He hoped his boy got some negotiating mileage out of this, another desperado in his gene pool.

Susan was mingling nicely, butterfly-like.

She'd asked Buckley what the whirlybird visit was about, he'd said it was on a mission of mercy, and she gave him one of her you're-drinking-this-time-of-the-day-again looks.

Beth's dad Chuck and his young wife, Heather, made the scene. Chuck and Heather were in aloha shirts and white shorts, both outfits several sizes too small. On her, it was a perfect fit. Heather was making a desperate effort to blend in with Beth and her egghead pals, and vice versa. There were lockjaw smiles all around.

Buckley kept a close, fatherly eye on his daughter-in-law and her delicate condition. She looked — what was the word they used? — radiant.

Yeah, radiant.

*I got a secret. My boy knocked up his girl friend. I'm gonna be a grandpa.*

Buckley jumped and clicked his heels together, startling a nearby table of propellerheads, one of whom dribbled white wine down his chin.

Chuck sidled up to Buckley, said the grub looked and smelled great, and asked what he was drinking.

"Belikin."

Chuck had finished his beer, crushed the can in his hand, and licked his lips. "Good suds?"

The insulated sack was at Buckley's feet, the exclusive property of him and his boy. He slid it away from the Chuckster.

"Yep. Very."

"Never heard of it. Where's it made?"

"Belize."

"That's one of those former Soviets or Yugoslavias?"

Buckley said it wasn't and told Chuck where Belize was.

"Oh yeah, I've been down there."

"You have?"

"Puerto Vallarta in Mexico. Heather and me honeymooned in P.V. You can have it. Riding in from the airport, the poverty, those shacks, chickens in and out of them. We stuck close to the resort, the pool and the beach."

"There's always Disneyland," Buckley said, laying on more thighs and breasts that instantly sizzled.

Chuck gazed at Buckley's face for confirmation he'd been insulted, but Buckley's eyes had been on his food throughout.

"That's good beer?"

"Very," Buckley repeated.

"Won't it get warm like that?"

"I'm keeping up," Buckley said, giving him a stink eye that said touch my F-day gift and they'll be calling you Nine Finger Charlie. "Don't you worry."

Chuck drifted off to become unwanted elsewhere.

Bud Pogue appeared at Buckley's side in a Bart Simpson T-shirt, radioactive blue Bermudas, a beer in one hand, a cigarette in the other. His was the only smoke Buckley had smelled other than what he was generating.

"What are you so happy about, Buckley?"

"Happy?"

"You're whistling."

"Yeah. Guess I was."

"Off key."

"You a talent scout too, Pogue? Whistling while you work, it's an old tradition."

"Let's do us some word association," Pogue said.

"Shoot."

"Cuba."

"Cuba?"

"I got me a head's up from a source. I was erroneous

when I said nobody was interested in your hide."

Pogue paused until Buckley's expression properly sobered.

"To give you a historical context, we've had a corncob up our butts regarding Cuba for in excess of forty years. Castro's outlasted eight U.S. Presidents, from Ike to Clinton. You haven't really been to Cuba, have you?"

"Never in a million years."

"Thanks to the nitwits on that TV program, that statement is in severe doubt. The State and Justice Departments are in a minor uproar. You mucking about in the U.S. of A. after consorting with Fidel, well, these are piddly little gripes, but somebody tosses a net over you, somebody's career is made."

Buckley turned some thighs. "Thanks for the tip."

"You don't believe me."

"Sure I do."

"They're building you up as an agent."

"I don't think you mean as an insurance or real estate agent."

"Secret agent. Spy."

"I've never even voted."

"Listen, Buckley, I've had my ear to the ground in that neighborhood for a good long while. They have these anti-trust busybodies at Justice who been sticking their noses into Mr. B's business."

Buckley looked at him.

Pogue raised his right hand, his cigarette like a torch. "Scout's honor. Just between you and me and the gatepost, I'm gearing up to snoop where these Justice bulldogs have been dipping their wicks into in event of a warrant or a special prosecutor or any of that chickenshit hardball nonsense. Mr. B doesn't know and he ain't gonna know, not from me."

"Blackmailing them, not that I'm criticizing?"

"Merely reaching into the closet and rattling skeletons."

"My boy, is he gonna have a government problem?"

"Not if me and the legal department can help it. Nothing stalling tactics and dirty pool can't delay till Mr. B's hair is as thin and gray like yours. One way or another, though, a shitstorm is a' brewing. Which reminds me, I nailed that little dildo who put the wheels on our server."

"The server, right? In that bar?"

"One and the same. Sitting outside in a truck, him and the machine, waiting on his buyer. He sold me his soul instead and I saved him from romance in the jailhouse shower room. Wanna hear the dirty details."

"No."

"I'm not bullshitting you on the Cuba flap, Buckley. Bright and early tomorrow morning, the machinery lurches into motion. Itinerary *numero uno*, I'm betting, is Andrew. He'll roll over in five minutes flat. When they're through, he'll have them believing Amelia Earhart's mummified corpse is in your steamer trunk and Sirhan Sirhan's on your Rolodex."

"You wouldn't be trying to be rid of me, would you?"

Pogue chuckled. "Oh, I get it."

"Get what?"

"Me and Dotti, you as my competition."

Buckley said nothing.

"I wanna clear the air on that situation. Tell my tale regarding me and her."

"Last time I kissed and told, I was fourteen years old and lying," Buckley said.

"Dotti's a sweet gal but not worth a chronic nicotine fit, but we might've clicked despite her faults. We were one drink away from her making a one-night stand out of me, two drinks max. We liked each other's voices on the phone when we first talked and jelled from there."

"Amazing," Buckley said, squinting into the flare-up he raised by turning chicken skin side down.

"I understand diddly-squat about gals, Buckley, but I understand one rock-hard fact. The difference between men and women is that women know in their heart of hearts they can change people, especially guys, if they work long and hard enough at it.

"Guys know that this is impossible. It is in the same realm of likelihood as the perpetual motion machine and making gold outta lead. Blessed by this faulty premise, I attract ladies who wanna make a project out of me."

Cigarette in mouth, freeing a hand, Pogue ticked off the reasons on his fingers, "My drinking, my smoking, my language, how I dress, how I drive."

Buckley considered himself as much of a project as Bud Pogue. Yet Dotti Magnuson had not indicated the slightest desire to jump his bones or reform him. He was mildly hurt, but no longer jealous.

"How does that work out for them, Pogue, the projects?"

He shrugged. "Ask my ex-wives. Dotti and me, I'd shut off the ignition in the motel parking lot. Thought I'd hit the home run ball. Then she went and got a sudden headache. We went to the airport instead. She must've decided some projects are tougher than others. Some impossible. Her last drink, I should of ordered a double for her."

"Well, thanks for the tip. I'll be leaving shortly."

"Just hauling ass back to Belize?"

Buckley nodded. "That's the simplest for everyone concerned."

"You got my approval and not only because I think you're a selfish, immature prick who shares a number of my qualities if you can call them that, which is why I'm constantly pissed whenever I'm within fifty meters of your sorry ass."

Buckley smiled. "Glad to be making your day."

"You're how old if you don't object to me asking?"

"I object. Sixty."

"Not turning over a new leaf, are you?"

"Nope."

Pogue gave him a comradely punch to the shoulder.

"Attaboy. I'm aspiring that when I'm your age, I'll of stuck to my standards too."

"Keep up the good work," said Buckley.

# 22.

Joe Buckley, climbing to 33,000 feet, nestled in first class leather, practiced his own signature.

"How'm I doing?" he asked Susan. "Just Philip has lousy handwriting and I think he spelled Buckley wrong on the dotted line."

"Will you keep that on your lap under the tray," she hissed.

"You sound just like Just Philip," Buckley said.

"I don't want to hear about your lowlife, criminal friends, nor do I care to meet them."

"Just Philip and I aren't friends. We do business together is all."

The flight attendant brought drinks and lunch menus. They were bound for Belize City, on the Seattle-to-Houston leg.

Buckley had bought his own coach ticket, but Susan upgraded him to First, not divulging the cost, saying that it was her Father's Day present to him.

He had $28 in his wallet and to his name. If his pride had muscled into the transaction, he'd be by his lonesome, back in steerage.

Susan had seen him off at the airport, but surprising him by boarding too, explaining that she needed a vacation, that Irene could cool her jets regarding the coach house. As they departed the Buckley property, she had spotted a sedan behind them with U.S. Government plates. He said it was a coincidence. She asked why was its blinker on at our driveway, then?

He said, hey, ships passing in the night. Buckley was

so close to touching Belizean soil that his paranoia had completely rolled off him.

"If I'm not home to be grilled, I don't have to take the Fifth," she had said. "I don't have the stomach to lie to a federal employee who isn't IRS."

"Seriously, is my signature good or bad or indifferent?"

"I'm not going to be near you when we go through any lines, Joe. I mean it."

"Wouldn't ask you to, for Chrissake. The signature?"

"You're a fair to middling forger. The picture, though."

Buckley looked at the passport, then her. "I don't resemble him?"

"You do. You're both old and tired."

"That's it?"

"You look slippery. He looks like a solid citizen, whoever the gentleman is."

"He does look kind of dull," Buckley agreed.

"Please get it out of sight. Now."

Buckley stuffed the passport into a pocket. "Nobody hassles me. What am I worried about?"

"That's the spirit." Susan unlocked a brand-new diary book.

Buckley watched, recalling how she kept the key of her current journal on a fine gold necklace chain. "I didn't once peek."

"I know you didn't, Joe."

"You can pick those locks with a paper clip, you know," Buckley said.

The flight attendant returned for their orders. He selected the filet, rare, extra butter for the garlic mashed potatoes and asparagus, and another cold beer. She had the pasta, some fancy Euro name he couldn't pronounce and a glass of red wine.

"They're your arteries," she said, unzipping her carry-on, pulled out a laptop, and booted up. She skimmed a page and began typing.

"Just like the yuppies," Buckley said.

Susan continued typing.

"You refused to write in your diary in front of me."

"Or anybody else. This isn't a diary entry. It's the outline of an outline of a rough draft. It's perhaps, perhaps, perhaps the start of a romance novel. Everybody who knows my diary prose says I should write one, and everybody does, thanks to Andrew."

"What's it about?"

"Authors don't reveal their plot lines," Susan said, typing faster. "It's bad luck."

"Don't stick me in Cuba smoking stogies with Fidel. I haven't set a single, solitary foot on Cuban soil."

"Don't flatter yourself. It's not about you. It's fiction, not an autobiography."

"Sure, Sooz."

"Okay, not too autobiographical."

After five minutes, her typing and the hum of the jet engines was all the silence Buckley could tolerate. "So how long does it take to write a romance novel?"

"I haven't the foggiest."

"Your vacation is gonna be spent writing a book?"

"I'm pulling a Joseph J. Buckley. I'll play it by ear," she said. "Today, on an irrational urge, I bought a ticket and stepped on to an airplane. Tomorrow, who knows?"

"You hadn't planned this ahead?"

"No sir."

"You happened to have your passport on you and a bag packed in the car."

"After last night and the night before, it might have crossed my unconscious mind. I was simply being prepared for uncharacteristic behavior on my part."

"I'm damn glad it did. The thing is, book writers take

years to write books, don't they?"

"Your actual question is, how long am I planning on staying. Again, the answer is that I haven't the foggiest."

"You could shack up with me. We could discuss the issue in that particular venue."

"This is the cubbyhole room with a shared bath down the hall?"

"It's efficient. Clean too."

"No thanks. Besides, you'll be busy organizing your tour guide business."

"Correct."

"I could finance —"

"Nope."

"Excuse me. Buckley's Law: I don't take advantage of women."

"For money," he said. "Words to live by."

"I can be a silent partner. I have to take the investment plunge eventually. This staggering wealth, Joe, I can't cope. It's the same reason I don't buy lotto tickets. I didn't want money I didn't deserve to turn my life inside out."

Listening to the *thunk-thunk-thunk* of Susan's keyboard, Buckley peered out at blue sky above and cloud dumplings below.

"We'll talk later on the subject. Your dough's not going anywhere and I'll catch on fast when I hang out my shingle. This'll be a business I can expand if I can find qualified assistants. It's surefire old age security, better late than never.

"I know people and my life list is up to two ninety-seven. What the hell, I'll round it off to three hundred. That'll attract hardcore birders, the Audubon Society folks. I'll take people to Tikal in Guatemala. Who knows, maybe even Copan. That's a big-league ruin in Honduras."

"You have Dotti Magnuson's documents?"

"Yep. Which I'll check over at my earliest opportunity."

"Sun and sand and sea," Susan said. "When I'm not writing, can you arrange that, Mr. Tour Guide?"

"San Pedro out on Ambergris Caye. A fifteen-minute puddle jumper flight out of Belize City. The cayes have it all."

"Sun?"

"Without lotion, you'll be a lobster in an hour. But this time of year, you'll have a little afternoon shower to cool things off."

"How little?"

"Hardly ever in excess of an inch. Or two."

"Sea?"

"Warm as bathwater."

"Sand?"

"Like granulated sugar."

"Sold."

"How long?"

"A week, then inland to see you for a day or two, but — please don't take this the wrong way — not in your crackerbox."

"There are some nice hotels in San Ignacio. I'll book you. Us."

"My practical side is informing me that I should be home after two weeks at the most, to make a decision on a new place and see how Beth is doing."

"Have I told you I was the first to know that our boy knocked her up out of wedlock?"

"For only the fifty-seventh time."

"I'm concerned about them on a different situation too." Buckley leaned in and whispered. "Between you, me and the gatepost, at the barbecue Bud Pogue saying the Justice Department trust-busters are poking their noses into sjbWare, it's got me worried."

"And that Bud was going to counterpunch and gather *flagrante delicto* material on their investigators?"

"Is that French for pants down around your knees and flashbulbs going off?"

Susan nodded, laughing.

"Joe, that's old news. Bud, bless him, is a blowhard in constant search of windmills to tilt. I wouldn't worry about Stanley and sjbWare. These inquiries are very preliminary and unofficial. His level of success attracts resentment. He's been on the up-and-up his entire life. Why, he didn't even lie to me about cleaning his room or doing his homework."

"Amazing job you did with him, Sooz. He didn't inherit those traits from me."

"Stanley is leaving as we speak to visit Taylor Smyth."

"I've been writing him a letter in my head," Buckley said. "I've gotten as far as Dear Mr. Smyth."

"Don't force it, Joe. It'll come."

"Answer me a question. How come Stan-ley and Beth dress like twins?"

"The law of averages," Susan said. "Your son is no clotheshorse. It was a bone of contention between us when he was growing up. He resented the bother of clothes shopping and didn't care what I bought him. Beth's the same."

"That's unusual for a gal. What do they wear in the winter?"

"Sweatshirts."

"You're coming back to Belize after your house deal is done and checking in on the kids, I mean for an encore visit, aren't you? There's a zillion things to do and see."

"Could be, especially if the setting inspires my novel."

"It will, no doubt. Who're you gonna sell it to when you're done?"

"Good question. The competition is so intense, the odds are stacked against a new novelist breaking in."

"Why not just buy yourself a book publishing house?

You can pick you own authors."

Susan lifted her fingers from the keys and pursed her lips. "Now there's a possibility. This is your laptop, incidentally, an early Merry Christmas to you from me. You can use it to e-mail your son and daughter-in-law and ex-wife and future grandchild. You can be a positive influence on Stanley."

Buckley's eyes widened. "Me, a *positive* influence?"

"By attempting to squelch his obsession with your brother."

If Susan knew he was going to sign a paper permitting the boy to dig up Big Stan, she'd have a cow.

"I intend to work on the problem. I'll be proactive as all get-out. It's been bugging me too. Remember our billiard parlor incident?"

"That shall not be forgotten quickly."

"Well, the longer I think about it, the more I'm convinced our boy knew the odds were high those weasels would be there and that something would happen by virtue of him making the scene. He had something to prove to himself, to me, to his dead Uncle Stan."

She offered him the laptop. "Thanks in advance for what you can do, Joe. Care for a lesson before lunch is served? We'll start learning a little keyboarding skill, starting at qwerty."

"Maybe later, Sooz. I can't keyboard on an empty stomach."

"Stanley is a card-carrying member of the digital generation, Joe. You get his attention in his medium. Digital photography is in its infancy. You can upload and download nature photos if you wish. You've transferred money online. You're already halfway to computer literacy."

"Hah. I'm a slow learner in certain areas," Buckley said. "You'll definitely have to make another trip or three to tutor me."

Susan looked at him. "I probably love you to death and always have and always will."

"Ditto," Buckley said, kissing her.

"But I am not going to be on a ball and chain. Holy matrimony and I are through. *Fini.*"

"Likewise," Buckley said with an exaggerated sigh of relief. "Amen."

She smiled. "I wouldn't say yes if you dropped to your knees and proposed."

"Who the hell's proposing? I look like I've lost my marbles? I'm propositioning."

Their meals were served. That last point settled, they ate with great appetite, and went on to live happily ever after.

Thank you for reading.

Please review this book. Reviews help other s find Absolutely Amazing eBooks and inspire us to keep providing these marvelous tales.

If you would like to be put on our email list to receive updates on new releases, contests, and promotions, please go to AbsolutelyAmazingEbooks.com and sign up.

# Meet the Author

A prolific author, Gary Alexander has written 16 novels, including *Loot,* fourth in the mystery series featuring comic Buster Hightower. *Disappeared*, the first in the series, has been optioned to Universal Studios.

He's written 150+ short stories and sold travel articles to 6 major dailies. One story appeared in *Best American Mystery Stories 2010*, another in *Ice Cold*, last year's Mystery Writers of America anthology.

Alexander is a nonsmoking, nondrinking vegetarian. He does, however, abuse caffeine and chocolate.

# The New
# Atlantian Library

New AtlantianLibrary.com
or AbsolutelyAmazingEbooks.com
or AA-eBooks.com

www.ingramcontent.com/pod-product-compliance
Lightning Source LLC
Chambersburg PA
CBHW061454030726
47503CB00005B/1702